William Brisbane Dick

Dick's speeches for tiny tots

William Brisbane Dick

Dick's speeches for tiny tots

ISBN/EAN: 9783743376960

Manufactured in Europe, USA, Canada, Australia, Japa

Cover: Foto ©Andreas Hilbeck / pixelio.de

Manufactured and distributed by brebook publishing software
(www.brebook.com)

William Brisbane Dick

Dick's speeches for tiny tots

3

TINY TOTS.

PROLOGUE.

FOR A TINY TOT.

I am only a little child, and I am afraid I cannot speak loud enough to make you all hear me—it is so hard to talk to so many people.

They say little children should be seen and not heard; but that does not mean smart little ones like *me*.

I know you are all nice, kind people, or else you would not have come to hear as well as see us tonight, and we thank you all very much for coming. How do you like my little speech?

ROBIN REDBREAST'S SECRET.

I have a secret I would like
  The little girls to know;
But I won't tell a single boy—
  They rob the poor birds so.
We have four pretty little nests;
  We watch them with great care;
Full fifty eggs are in this tree—
  Don't tell the boys they're there.

Joe Thompson robbed the nest last year,
  And year before, Tom Brown;
I'll tell it loud as I can sing
  To every one in town.
Swallow and sparrow, lark and thrush,
  Will tell you just the same;
To make us all so sorrowful,
  It is a wicked shame.

WHAT SHE SAID.

She tole me sumfin defful !
  It almost made me cry !
I never will b'lieve it—
  It *mus'* be all a lie ! —
I mean, she mus' be 'staken.
  I know she b'oke my heart;

I never can forgive her,
   That horrid Maggie Start!

Tuesdays she does her bakin's;
   An' so I fought, you see,
I'd make some fimble cookies
   For Arabella's tea.
An' so I took my dollies
   An' set 'em in a row,
Where they could oversee me
   When I mixed up my dough.

An' when I'd wolled an' mixed it
   Free minutes or an hour,
Somehow I dwopped my woller,
   An' spilt a lot of flour.
An' I was defful firsty,
   An' fought I'd help myself
To jes' a little dwop of milk
   Off from the pantry shelf.

So I weached up on tiptoe;
   But, quicker than a flash,
The horrid pan turned over,
   An' down it came, kersplash!
Oh, then you should have seen her
   Rush frough that pantry door!
"An' *this* is where you be!" she said;
   "Oh, what a lookin' floor!

" You an' your dolls—I'll shake you all;
  I'll shake you black 'n' blue ! "
" You shall not touch us, miss," I cried;
  " We're jest as good as you !
An' I will tell my mofer
  The minute she gets home ;
An' I will tell ole Santa Claus,
  An' I'll tell every one."

Oh, then you should have heard her laugh !
  " Tell Santa Claus, indeed !
I'd like to have you find him first—
  The humbug never lived ! "
" What do you mean, you Maggie Start ?
  Is dear old Santa dead ? "
" Old Santa *never lived*," she cried—
  And *that* is what she said.

ALL THINGS.

All things bright and beautiful,
  All things great and small,
All things wise and wonderful—
  Our Father made them all.

Each little flower that opens,
  Each little bird that sings—
He made their lovely colors,
  He made their tiny wings.

He gave us *eyes* to *see* them,
  And *lips* that we might tell
How *good* is God our Father,
  Who doeth *all things well.*

FLO'S LETTER.

A sweet little baby brother
  Had come to live with Flo;
And she wanted it brought to the table,
  Where it might eat and grow.

" It must wait awhile," said grandma,
  In answer to her plea,
" For a little thing that hasn't teeth
  Can't eat like you and me."

" Why! hasn't it got teeth, grandma ? "
  Asked Flo, in great surprise;
" Oh my ! but isn't it funny—
  No teeth, but nose and eyes!

" I guess "—after thinking gravely—
  " They must have been forgot;
Can't we buy him some like grandpa ?
  I'd like to know why not ? "

That afternoon in the corner,
  With paper, pen, and ink,
Went Flo, saying, " Don't talk to me ;
  If you do, you'll 'sturb my think.

"I am writing a letter, grandma,
  To send away to-night;
And 'cause it's very 'portant,
  I want to get it right."

At last the letter was finished—
  A wonderful thing to see,
And directed to "God in heaven."
  "Please read it over to me,"

Said little Flo to her grandma,
  "To see if it's right, you know."
And here is the letter written
  To God by little Flo:

"Dear God! the baby you brought us
  Is awful nice and sweet;
But because you forgot his toofies
  The poor little thing can't eat.

"That's why I am writing this letter
  A purpose to let you know;
Please come and finish the baby.
  That's all, from little Flo."

PICCANINNY LULLABY.

I see a gray coon in de corn;
  Sleep, baby, sleep.
I heah de mastah blow his horn;
  Sleep, baby, sleep.

I see a niggah at de gray coon shoot,
I heah de echo of de ole horn's toot,
An' I heah an owl in de wild-wood hoot;
    Sleep, baby, sleep.

A 'gator's gruntin' in de ole bayou—
    Sleep, baby, sleep—
At a fat pig crawfishin' in de flue;
    Sleep, baby, sleep.
His teeth am big an' wide an' white,
An' he am chucklin' at de great big bite
He's gwine to hab outen dat pig to-nite;
    Sleep, baby, sleep.

I heah de wild geese flyin' by;
    Sleep, baby, sleep.
De air am ringin' wid dere cry;
    Sleep, baby, sleep.
It's gwine to be cole, but you am snug
As de hoppin' lizard an' de little June-bug,
So I'll leabe you now wid a good-nite hug;
    Sleep, baby, sleep.

THE RAINDROPS.

"I'm going down to cheer a flower,"
  Cried a little drop of rain;
"I hear it sigh; it droops its head,
  As if in weary pain!"

"And I will go!"   "And I!"   "And I!"
    Cried all the raindrops near;
So down they went in merry haste
    The whole wide field to cheer.

The drooping flowers looked up and smiled;
    The whole wide field was glad—
Fresh water-cups for thirsty lips
    Each happy flower had.

And when the sun came shining out,
    The raindrops in his face
Sparkled and laughed, till, radiantly,
    A rainbow arched the place!

OUR FLAG.

Shout for the banner bright
Unfurling in the light—
    Our country's flag.
Shout till each rugged hill,
Each valley, low and still,
Shall echo—Lord, we will
    Protect our flag.

Weep for the flag once borne
Through blood and shame, and torn—
    Our noble flag!

God, for these glorious days
Of peace receive our praise;
Blest Guide of all our ways,
    Protect our flag.

MAY.

Pretty little violets, waking from your sleep,
Fragrant little blossoms, just about to peep,
Would you know the reason all the world is gay?
Listen to the bobolink telling you 'tis May.

Little ferns and grasses, all so green and bright,
Purple clover nodding, daisies fresh and white,
Would you know the reason all the world is gay?
Listen to the bobolink telling you 'tis May.

Darling little warblers, coming in the spring,
Would you know the reason that you love to sing?
Hear the merry children shouting as they play,
" Listen to the bobolink telling us 'tis May!"

MARGARET'S BROKEN SLATE.

I've b'oken my slate!
    Oh! what s'all I do?
Papa's thus b'ot it,
    So p'etty and new!

And me could draw ho'ses
  And w'ite, when me try;
But now slate is b'oken,
  So des I will ky.

Oh no, I won't neder—
  I 'member one day
I hurted my fin'er
  While I was at play;

And mama took sumfin—
  'Twas arn'ca, I tink—
And den my poor fin'er
  Was cured in a wink.

So I'll wun to mama,
  And take her my slate,
To give it some arn'ca
  Before it's too late.

HIS PROFESSION.

My boy and I rode in the train,
  One morning bright and clear;
"When I'm a grown-up man," said he,
  "I'll be an engineer!"
But soon the dust flew in his eyes.
  And heavy grew his head;

"I wouldn't be an engineer
  For all the world!" he said.

My boy was at a seaport town,
  And saw the rolling sea;
"Mama," he said, one evening,
  "A sailor I shall be!"
We took him to a yacht-race—
  He had to go to bed!
"I wouldn't be a sailor now
  For all the world!" he said.

We read him stirring stories
  Of soldiers and their fame;
"I'll go and fight," cried Freddie,
  "And put them all to shame!"
We told him of a soldier's life;
  He shook his little head;
"I wouldn't be a soldier now
  For all the world!" he said.

And thus to each profession
  He first said "yes," then "no."
"To make a choice is hard," he said;
  "At least, *I* find it so."
"But what, then, will you be," I asked,
  "When you are grown up, Fred?"
"I really think I'll only be
  A gentleman," he said.

LITTLE THINGS.

MOTION SONG.

We are leaflets, growing, growing;
　　Here's a cloud and there's the sun.
Now the rain is soaking, soaking;
　　We are dripping, every one.

(*Chorus.*)

But we grow, we grow, we grow,
Yes, we all are growing.
　　(*Chorus repeated after each stanza.*)

We are flowers, growing, growing,
　　Dancing when the wind comes by,
Turning as the sunlight circles,
　　Drooping heads when night is nigh.

We are cotton, growing, growing,
　　Golden flowers glittering;
Some day great white bolls shall open
　　For the angels' harvesting.

We are nestlings, growing, growing,
　　Open beak and fluttering wing;
Now we need a mother's tending,
　　Some day in the sky we'll sing.

We are seedling acorns, pushing
　　Warm leaves from the brown, soft sand;
Wide and far and high and leafy,
　　Great oak-trees some day we'll stand.

We are little raindrops, dripping,
  Dropping, falling from the cloud;
Some day in the thunderous ocean
  You shall hear our voices loud.

We are infant scholars, saying
  A by B and B by C;
Some day we'll be saints in heaven,
  Learning God's great mystery.

OVER THE BARE HILLS.

Over the bare hills, far away,
Somebody's traveling day by day;
Coming so slowly—I wonder why !
Oh, she is busy as she goes by.

"Sing, little brook; wake up and hear !
Where is the song that you learned last year ?
Don't you remember the dear old tune ?
Naughty small brook, to forget so soon !

" Dainty wee clouds in the bright blue sky,
Last year I taught you to float so high !
Flowers, where are you ? Why don't you blow ?
Come, Dandelion, you can, you know.

"Spring up, tall grasses and daisies and clover;
Last year I taught you how, over and over;
Come with me, every one—this is the way;
Don't you remember me ? Why, I am May."

NOT GEORGE WASHINGTON.

I saw him standing in the crowd,
    A comely youth and fair;
There was a brightness in his eye,
    A glory in his hair!
I saw his comrades gaze on him—
    His comrades standing by;
I heard them whisper each to each,
    " He never told a lie !"

I thought of questions very hard
    For boys to answer right—
" How did you tear those pantaloons ? "
    " My son, what caused the fight ? "
" Who left the gate ajar last night ? "
    " Who bit the pumpkin pie ? "
What boy could answer all of these
    And never tell a lie ?

I proudly took him by the hand—
    My words with praise were rife;
I blessed that boy who never told
    A falsehood in his life;
I told him I was proud of him.
    A fellow standing by
Informed me that *that* boy was dumb
    Who never told a lie.

GRUMBLE CORNER AND THANKSGIVING STREET.

I knew a man whose name was Horner,
Who used to live on Grumble Corner—
Grumble Corner, in Cross Patch Town—
And was never seen without a frown.
He grumbled at this, he grumbled at that;
He growled at the dog, he growled at the cat;
He grumbled at morning, he grumbled at night;
And to grumble and growl were his chief delight.

He grumbled so much at his wife that she
Began to grumble as well as he;
And all the children, wherever they went,
Reflected their parents' discontent.
If the sky was dark and betokened rain,
Then Mr. Horner was sure to complain;
And if there was never a cloud about,
He'd grumble because of a threatened drought.

His meals were never to suit his taste;
He grumbled at having to eat in haste;
The bread was poor, or the meat was tough,
Or else he hadn't had half enough.
No matter how hard his wife might try
To please her husband, with scornful eye
He'd look around, and then, with a scowl
At something or other, begin to growl.

One day, as I loitered along the street,
My old acquaintance I chanced to meet,
Whose face was without the look of care
And the ugly frown that it used to wear.
" I may be mistaken, perhaps," I said,
As, after saluting, I turned my head ;
" But it is, and it isn't, the Mr. Horner
Who lived so long on Grumble Corner ! "

I met him next day, and I met him again,
In melting weather, in pouring rain,
When stocks were up, and when stocks were down ;
But a smile somehow had replaced the frown.
It puzzled me much ; and so, one day,
I seized his hand in a friendly way,
And said, " Mr. Horner, I'd like to know
What has happened to change you so ? "

He laughed a laugh that was good to hear,
For it told of a conscience calm and clear ;
And he said, with none of the old-time drawl,
" Why, I've changed my residence—that is all ! "
" Changed your residence ? " " Yes," said Horner ;
" It wasn't healthy on Grumble Corner,
And so I moved—'twas a change complete ;
And you'll find me now on Thanksgiving Street."

Now every day, as I move along
The streets so filled with the busy throng,

I watch each face, and can always tell
Where men and women and children dwell;
And many a discontented mourner
Is spending his days on Grumble Corner,
Sour and sad, whom I long to entreat
To take a house on Thanksgiving Street.

A COMPLAINT.

A BOY'S RECITATION.

I think it really mean—don't you ?—
To leave us nothing at all to do !
In a world all made to order so .
A modern boy has no earthly show.

Columbus sailed across the sea—
Which might have been done by you or me—
And now they call him great and wise,
They praise his genius and enterprise,
Although when he found our native land
He took it for India's coral strand !

There's Newton, too, saw an apple fall
Down from the branch, and that was all;
Yet they talk of his great imagination,
And say he discovered gravitation.
Goodness me ! why, I could have told
Him all about it ; at ten years old
I knew why things fell, and I studied the rule
For " falling bodies " in grammar-school !

There's noble George, who wouldn't lie—
Perhaps he couldn't; he didn't try.
But if I should cut down a cherry-tree,
My father would only laugh at me.

Benjamin Franklin—what did *he* do?
Flew a big kite—on Sunday, too;
Standing out in a heavy shower
Getting soaked for half an hour,
Fishing for lightning with a string,
To see if he couldn't bottle the thing.
Suppose I should fly my kite in the rain?
People would say that I wasn't sane.
Why should there such a difference be
Between Ben Franklin, Esq., and me?

Then there's Napoleon First, of France:
Suppose that we had had his chance,
No doubt we'd have been emperors too;
But we'd have conquered at Waterloo.
I wouldn't have had old Grouchy make
Such a stupid and grave mistake;
I should have sent him the proper way
To arrive in time to save the day!

Still, what makes me feel the worst
Is Adam's renown for being first.
That was easy enough, you know—
It was just a thing that happened so.

And my sister says, " If it had been *me*,
I wouldn't have touched the apple-tree."
That's so.   If she sees a snake to-day
She gives a scream and scoots away.

To write such things as Shakespeare's plays
Was not so hard in Queen Bess's days;
But now, when everything has been done,
I cannot think of a single one
To bring a boy to wealth and fame—
It's a regular, downright, burning shame !

EPILOGUE.

FOR A TOT.

Before we say good-by, I want to tell you that I
love you all very much.   You know who it was that
loved little ones like me, and wanted us to come to
Him ; and I am sure you cannot help loving us little
ones too, almost as much as He did.

It is because I am little that I love you all.   You
know, when I get big I shall have to love a few
people more, and other people less ; and when I get
married I shall have to love one person more than *all*
the rest.   So you ought to be very glad that I am little
and can love you all so much.   And now I blow you
all a good-by kiss.

DECEMBER.

On Christmas day, when fires were lit,
   And all our breakfasts done,
We spread our toys out on the floor,
   And played there in the sun.

The nursery smelled of Christmas tree,
   And under where it stood
The shepherds watched their flocks of sheep—
   All made of painted wood.

Outside the house the air was cold,
   And quiet all about,
Till far across the snowy roofs
   The Christmas bells rang out.

But soon the sleigh-bells jingled by
   Upon the street below,
And people on the way to church
   Went crunching through the snow.

We did not quarrel once all day;
   Mama and grandma said
They liked to be in where we were,
   So pleasantly we played.

I do not see how any child
   Is cross on Christmas day,
When all the lovely toys are new,
   And every one can play.

AN INDIGNANT SCHOLAR.

Such a horrid jogafry lesson !
   Cities and mountains and lakes,
And the longest, crookedest rivers,
   Just wriggling about like snakes.
I tell you I wish Columbus
   Hadn't heard the earth was a ball,
And started to find new countries
   That folks didn't need at all.

Now wouldn't it be too lovely
   If all that you had to find out
Was just about Spain and England,
   And a few other lands thereabout;
And the rest of the maps were printed
   With pink and yellow, to say,
" *All this is an unknown region,*
   Where bogies and fairies stay ? "

But what is the use of wishing,
   Since Columbus sailed over here,
And men keep hunting and 'sploring
   And finding things every year ?
Now show me the Yampa River,
   And tell me where does it flow ?
And how do you bound Montana,
   And Utah and Mexico ?

A LITTLE FELLER.

Say, Sunday's lonesome fur a little feller,
  With pop an' ma'am a-readin' all the while,
An' never sayin' anythin' to cheer ye,
  An' lookin' 's if they didn't know how to smile;
With hook an' line a-hangin' in the woodshed,
  An' lots o' 'orms down by the outside cellar,
An' Brown's Creek just over by the mill-dam—
  Say, Sunday's lonesome fur a little feller.

Why, Sunday's lonesome fur a little feller
  Right on from sun-up, when the day commences;
Fur little fellers don't have much to think of
  'Cept chasin' gophers 'long the corn-field fences,
Or diggin' after moles down in the wood-lot,
  Or climbin' after apples what's got meller,
Or fishin' down in Brown's Creek an' mill-pond—
  Say, Sunday's lonesome fur a little feller.

But Sunday's never lonesome fur a little feller
  When he is stayin' down to Uncle Ora's;
He took his book onct right out in the orchard,
  An' told us little chaps just lots o' stories—
All truly true, that happened once fur honest,
  An' one 'bout lions in a sort o' cellar,
An' how some angels came an' shut their mouths up,
  An' how they never teched that Dan'l feller.

An' Sunday's pleasant down to Aunt Marilda's;
  She lets us take some books that some one gin her,

An' takes us down to Sunday-school t' the school-
    house;
An' sometimes she has nice shortcake fur dinner,
And onct she had a puddin' full o' raisins,
    An' onct a frosted cake, all white an' yeller.
I think when I stay down to Aunt Marilda's
    That Sunday's pleasant fur a little feller.

WELCOME.

A CHILD'S SPEECH.

It scares me, my friends, to speak to you to-night.
My heart goes pittypat. I want to speak my piece,
and can scarce think what to say. Mine is a speech
of welcome. I am to say welcome to you all—right
welcome to our hall, our hearts, and to hear what we
have to say. Some of the larger boys who are study-
ing arithmetic and geography and grammar will make
believe they are orators or generals or kings; but I
don't. You all know me, and it's no use for me to
pretend to be what I am not; besides, I can welcome
you just as well just as I am; and now I say you are
just as welcome as you can be. Besides, we are real
glad you are here. We wondered if you would come,
we wanted you to come, we are glad you have come,
we thank you for your coming. Now you know you
are welcome.

Our speeches for to-night are not our **own.** The politicians, the lawyers, the speechmakers, among us are using the speeches made by great men before our day. We adopt theirs until we can make our own. Again, welcome.

GRANDMA.

When grandma puts her glasses on
  And looks at me just so,
If I have done a naughty thing,
  She's sure somehow to know.
How is it she can always tell
So very, very, very well ?

She says to me, " Yes, little one,
  'Tis written in your eye ! "
And if I look the other way,
  Or turn and seem to try
To hunt for something on the floor,
She's sure to know it all the more.

If I should put the glasses on
  And look in grandma's eyes,
Do you suppose that I should be
  So very, very wise ?
Now, what if I should find it true
That grandma had been naughty too !

THE QUARRELSOME KITTENS.

Two little kittens,
    One stormy night,
Began to quarrel,
    And then to fight.

One had a mouse,
    The other had none;
And that's the way
    The quarrel begun.

" *I'll* have that mouse,"
    Said the bigger cat.
" *You'll* have that mouse ?
    We'll *see* about that ! "

" I *will* have that mouse,"
    Said the eldest son ;
" You *sha'n't* have the mouse,"
    Said the little one.

The old woman seized
    Her sweeping-broom,
And swept both kittens
    Right out of the room.

The ground was all covered
    With frost and with snow ;
The two little kittens
    Had nowhere to go.

So they lay and shivered
  On a mat at the door,
While the old woman
  Was sweeping the floor.

And then they crept in,
  As quiet as mice,
All wet with the snow,
  And as cold as ice;

And found it much better,
  That stormy night,
To lie by the fire
  Than to quarrel and fight.

ROBIN'S NEW YEAR.

On the snowy branch of the holly-bush
  A gay little redbreast sings;
"Happy New Year to all, to all!" says he.
  Oh! loudly his greeting rings.
And in the warm nursery, way high up,
  From the window-pane looks down
A dear little girl with sunshiny hair,
  And a boy with eyes so brown.

To Robin they call, "Ho, ho! little bird,
  Why singing so gaily, pray?
The snow is so deep, the wind is so keen,
  You'll freeze with the cold to-day."

"Icicles hang on the mistletoe-bough,
  And snow on the meadow lies,
But I fear not the cold this New-Year's morn,"
  The brave little bird replies.

"For God He is good, and God He is love;
  He made the land and the sea ;
And the God that sees when the sparrows fall
  Will also take care of me."
Then he eats with a thankful heart the crumbs
  That the small white hands let fall,
And sings from his swing in the holly-bush,
  "Happy New Year to all, to all !"

THE GOLDEN KEY.

I know of a jeweled casket
  Where is hidden a golden key
That opens the door of a castle fair,
  Called the Castle of Courtesy.

Its owner, a bright-eyed maiden,
  When she wakes in the morning light,
Takes the treasure out from its hiding-place
  · And bears it around till night.

She opens the door of the castle
  With the beautiful golden key,
And smiles a welcome to all who come—
  Even strangers, like you and me.

And to every door in the castle
 The maiden fits her key;
Wide open it flies at her magic touch,
 That all may its treasures see.

The heart is the jeweled casket,
 And kindness the golden key
That opens the doors of the numberless rooms
 In the Castle of Courtesy.

NINETIETH PSALM.

Lord, Thou hast been our dwelling-place
 In generations past;
Before the mountains saw Thy face,
 Or earth in form was cast.

A thousand years before Thy sight
 Are but as yesterday,
Or as a watch-hour in the night,
 That hurrieth away.

As on a flood we all are borne,
 Our life is like a sleep;
Beneath Thine anger we must mourn,
 And for our sins must weep.

Our secret sins Thou bring'st to light,
 Our days pass quickly by;
They end in trouble, grief, and night,
 As onward cycles fly.

Oh, teach us to apply our days
   To wisdom's counsels pure,
And let Thy beauty and Thy praise
   Upon our works endure !

DOLLY'S BROKEN ARM.

Mama, do send for doctor-man,
   And tell him to be spry;
My dolly fell and broke her arm;
   I'm so afraid she'll die.

I thought that she was fast asleep,
   And laid her on the bed;
But down she dropped upon the floor;
   Oh dear ! she's almost dead !

Poor dolly! she was just as brave,
   And she did not cry at all.
Do you suppose she ever can
   Get over such a fall ?

But when the doctor mends her arm
   And wraps it up so tight,
Then I will be her little nurse,
   And watch with her all night.

And if she only will get well,
   And does not lose her arm,
I'll never let her fall again,
   Nor suffer any harm.

A CUP OF TEA.

A very old dame in a very small cot
Made tea in a blue-and-white Chinese tea-pot;
She drank it so black I'm sure you would think
'Twas the very worst thing an old lady could drink.
She never drank water, nor coffee, nor wine,
But said her black tea was exceedingly fine.
She'd draw it at morn, and at night drink it up
From an old-fashioned blue-and-white china tea-cup.
And she lived long ago, yet I have heard say
She's making and drinking her tea to this day.

"PLEASE, PREACHER-MAN, CAN I GO HOME?"

Bess went to church one sultry day;
She kept awake, I'm glad to say,
Till "fourthly" started on its way.

Then moments into hours grew;
Oh dear! oh dear! what should she do?
Unseen she glided from the pew,

And up the aisle demurely went,
On some absorbing mission bent,
Her eyes filled with a look intent.

She stopped and said, in plaintive tone,
With hand uplifted toward the dome,
"Please, preacher-man, can I go home?"

The treble voice, bell-like in sound,
Disturbed a sermon most profound;
A titter swelled as it went round.

A smile the pastor's face o'erspread;
He paused, and bent his stately head.
" Yes, little dear," he gently said.

THE LITTLE TOMTIT.

"Oh ! where do you come from, little Tomtit ? "
  " From birdland, of course," sang he.
He wasn't quite sure of the matter, I know,
  As he sat on the old oak-tree.

I asked him again: " Oh ! where do you live ? "
  " At Thomas Tit Hall," he cried.
" And what do you eat for your breakfast ? " said I.
  " A nice potted worm," he replied.

" And how do you dress in that little blue coat
  And nice yellow waistcoat so trim ? "
" They grow, little maiden," he cried, with a laugh.
  In wonder I gazed then at him.

" And how — " but he stopped me by saying, " My
      dear,
  I was taught, when a very young bird,
This sensible motto—I quote it to you:
  ' Little folks should be seen and not heard ' ! "

A GIRL'S ESSAY ON BOYS.

Boys are men that have not got as big as their papas; and girls are women that will be young ladies by and by.   Man was made before woman.   When God looked at Adam He said to Himself, "Well, I think I can do better if I try again;" and then He made Eve.   God liked Eve so much better than Adam that there have been more women than men. Boys are a trouble.   They wear out everything—but soap.   If I had my way, half the boys in the world would be girls, and the rest would be dolls.   My papa is so nice that I think he must have been a little girl when he was a little boy.

A BOY'S MOTHER.

My mother she's so good to me;
Ef I was good as I could be,
I couldn't be as good—no, sir!
Can't any boy be good as her!

She loves me when I'm glad er mad;
She loves me when I'm good er bad;
An', what's a funniest thing, she says
She loves me when she punishes.

I don't like her to punish me;
That don't hurt, but it hurts to see

Her cryin'—nen I cry; an' nen
We both cry—an' be good again.

She loves me when she cuts and sews
My little cloak and Sunday clothes;
An' when my pa comes home to tea
She loves him 'most as much as me.

She laughs an' tells him all I said,
An' grabs me up an' pats my head;
An' I hug her, an' hug my pa,
An' love him purt' nigh much as ma.

A LITTLE BOY'S VALENTINE.

Little girl across the way,
  You are so very sweet
I shouldn't be a bit surprised
  If you were good to eat.

Now what I'd like, if you would too,
  Would be to go and play—
Well, all the time, and all my life,
  On your side of the way.

I don't know anybody yet
  On your side of the street,
But often I look over there
  And watch you—you're so sweet.

When I am big, I tell you what,
  I don't care what they say,
I'll go across—and stay there, too—
  On your side of the way.

———————

A HOUSEKEEPER'S TROUBLES.

Dolly's wet her
Feet to get her
Posies, in the morning dew;
  Sure to be sick—
  Cold or colic—
Like as not the measles too.

There is Freddy,
Always ready
Into awful 'fairs to fall;
  Bad as Rosy—
  Doodness knows, I
Don't know how to manage 't all !

Jack or Norah's
Telled a story !
One or t'uver ate ma's cake !
  While there's silly,
  Greedy Willy
Got a drefful stomach-ache !

Naughty Bessie
Tored her dress; she
Wants anuver one, I s'pose;
    I tell you what,
    It tates a lot
Of work to teep my dolls in tose !

A LITTLE BOY'S PLEA.

Here I am most four feet high;
    I'm brimming full of fun;
I dance and whistle, laugh and sing,
    And hop and skip and run.

I suppose I bother big folks some
    With all my fun and glee;
But then remember, gentle folks,
    There is some work in me.

Five days each week I go to school—
    I'm very busy there;
And then of chores and errands, too,
    I always have my share.

So please don't scold me when I play,
    Although I make some noise;
It's hard to be so full of fun
    And still be quiet boys.

I am a little boy, you see;
  I never spoke before;
But if you'll listen to me now
  I'll tell you something more.

I'll tell you what I mean to be
  When I am grown a man:
I'll keep the store where letters come—
  I'll be the post-office man.

A TINY BOY'S SPEECH.

I am a very little boy,
  As you can plainly see;
And as I stand before you now
  I tremble in each knee.

But then I thought it would not do
  For all the boys in school
To make a speech and leave me out,
  Like a poor simple fool.

And so I plucked my courage up,
  Determined to be bold,
And have come out upon the stage
  To do as I am told.

I thank the ladies very much
  For listening to my speech;
And if they ask me, I am sure
  I'll give a kiss to each.

LITTLE WILLIE WARE.

"The night is cold," said Willie Ware;
  "A-coasting I will go."
He wore his father's sealskin cap,
  And lost it in the snow.

They searched the highland far and near,
  And Willie's pa was wild;
And then he got upon his ear,
  And interviewed that child.

And now, when Willie Ware comes round
  To stay with us a bit,
He will not take a chair.   He says
  He does not care to sit.

MY DOGGIE.

I have a little doggie,
  His back is smooth and white;
He has a ribbon round his neck,
  And wears it day and night.

He has a little basket
  All lined with Turkey red;
He often takes a little nap
  Before he goes to bed.

He stands upon his hind legs
  With sugar on his nose;
When I say "now" he snaps it up—
  What else did you suppose?

He has a bath on Mondays;
  Cook puts him in a tub,
And then with soap and flannel
  Begins to rub, rub, rub.

When I give him a penny,
  He goes to buy a bun;
He lays it down and barks quite loud
  Until the people come.

Now, isn't he a clever dog,
  And just as good as gold?
I think now I must stop and rest,
  Because my story's told.

"GRAN'MA AL'A'S DOES."

I wants to mend my wagon,
  And has to have some nails—
Jus' two free will be plenty—
  We're goin' to haul our rails;
The splendidest cob fences
  We're makin' ever was!

I wis' you'd help us find 'em—
  Gran'ma al'a's does.

My horse's name is Betsy;
  She jumped and broked her head ;
I put her in the stable,
  And fed her milk and bread.
The stable's in the parlor—
  We didn't make no muss;
I wis' you'd let her stay there—
  Gran'ma al'a's does.

I's goin' to the corn-field,
  To ride on Charley's plow;
I 'spect he'd like to have me;
  I wants to go just now.
Oh, won't I gee up awful,
  And whoa like Charley whoas !
I wis' you wouldn't bozzer—
  Gran'ma never does.

I wants some bread and butter—
  I's hungry worstest kind;
But Taddie mus'n't have none,
  'Cause she wouldn't mind.
Put plenty sugar on it;
  I tell you what, I knows
It's right to put on sugar—
  Gran'ma al'a's does.

A BOY'S APOLOGY.

I'd rather take a whipping now
Than stand up here and make a bow,
And speak before a crowd like this;
For much I fear you all may hiss.

But then I thought that Henry Clay
Had been a boy once in his day,
And Daniel Webster had to crawl
Before he ever walked at all.

"Large oaks from little acorns grow;"
And though I creep along quite slow,
Who knows but at some future day
I'll be as great a man as Clay?

Perhaps some lady here will say,
"That boy's too fast—take him away!"
This trouble I will save you now,
As thus I make my farewell bow.

WHAT I KNOW.

A very little boy am I,
And yet to speak I mean to try;
Because I know a thing or two,
As small as I appear to you.

I know that millers have fat hogs—
I've seen them roll about like logs;
But where the miller gets his corn
I never knew since I was born.

I know that lawyers oft get rich
When into people's suits they pitch;
But how they get the money paid
I never knew since I was made.

I know that doctors all dress fine,
No matter how their patients pine;
But how they get so much to spend
I never knew, you may depend.

I know the boys all love the girls,
And talk about their "eyes" and "curls";
But why the girls don't like a beau
I never do expect to know.

OUR FUTURE WORK.

RECITATION FOR TEN BOYS.

FIRST BOY..

Oh, what will be our future work? Come, boys, let's
choose a trade.
I'd like to be a *locksmith!* all the town would seek
my aid.

SIXTH BOY.

Across the waves, not *underneath*, my future path I'll
take !

I want to be a captain bold, like Raleigh or like
•   Drake ;

The captain of a bonny bark with sails so fair and
fleet—

From figurehead to keel she'll be so taut and trim
and neat !

I'll stand upon my bridge and shout, as forward still
we flee,

" *Starboard !* " or " *Port !* " or " *Land ahead !* " just as
the case may be.

SEVENTH BOY.

I'd like to be a *fireman*, with a helmet on my
head ;

You'll see me on my engine when the flames leap high
and red ;

When people call out " *Fire ! fire ! fire !* " and dread
fills all the town,

Oh, then you'll see me play my hose till flames die
hissing down !

But oh, remember there's a foe of deeper danger
near—

The raging drink does far more harm e'en than the
flames we fear !

EIGHTH BOY.

Oh, what will be our future work ?   I'm sure I cannot tell ;
But yet I think a *waiter's* life would suit me very
  well ;
In some bright temperance coffee-house (I'm glad
  there are so many)
I'd rush along with plate and dish, and thank you for
  your penny ;
I'd never, never fill your glass with drinks that hurt
  and harm—
I'll be a *temperance* waiter, with my napkin o'er my
  arm !

NINTH BOY.

And *I* will be a *druggist*, and your powders I'll pre-
  pare ;
I'll roll your pills and measure out your dose and
  draught with care ;
I'll mix the proper physic that's adapted to your
  case ;
I'll cure your headache, toothache, cough and cold,
  and swollen face !
Dear friends, I'll do my very best to cure your every
  pain,
And my advice to young and old will be just this—
  abstain !

SIXTH BOY.

Across the waves, not *underneath*, my future path I'll
    take !
I want to be a captain bold, like Raleigh or like
•   Drake ;
The captain of a bonny bark with sails so fair and
    fleet—
From figurehead to keel she'll be so taut and trim
    and neat !
I'll stand upon my bridge and shout, as forward still
    we flee,
" *Starboard !* " or " *Port !* " or " *Land ahead !* " just as
    the case may be.

SEVENTH BOY.

I'd like to be a *fireman*, with a helmet on my
    head ;
You'll see me on my engine when the flames leap high
    and red ;
When people call out " *Fire ! fire ! fire !* " and dread
    fills all the town,
Oh, then you'll see me play my hose till flames die
    hissing down !
But oh, remember there's a foe of deeper danger
    near—
The raging drink does far more harm e'en than the
    flames we fear !

EIGHTH BOY.

Oh, what will be our future work ?   I'm sure I cannot tell ;
But yet I think a *waiter's* life would suit me very
well ;
In some bright temperance coffee-house (I'm glad
there are so many)
I'd rush along with plate and dish, and thank you for
your penny ;
I'd never, never fill your glass with drinks that hurt
and harm—
I'll be a *temperance* waiter, with my napkin o'er my
arm !

NINTH BOY.

And *I* will be a *druggist*, and your powders I'll pre-
pare ;
I'll roll your pills and measure out your dose and
draught with care ;
I'll mix the proper physic that's adapted to your
case ;
I'll cure your headache, toothache, cough and cold,
and swollen face !
Dear friends, I'll do my very best to cure your every
pain,
And my advice to young and old will be just this—
abstain !

BEDTIME FANCIES.

Out from the corners and over the floor
    Come flocking and flocking the shadow band;
I will get in my little white coach and drive
    Through the Valley of Dreams into Slumberland.

I have four black horses that Night has lent;
    I call the name of my coachman Sleep;
And the little white coach is cozy and soft,
    As I nestle down in its cushions deep.

Heigh-ho! we are off.   The horses go slow
    At first, then fast and faster still,
With silent hoof-beats speeding on,
    Down to the foot of the Drowsy Hill.

This twilight place is the Valley of Dreams,
    Where all the wonderful dream things are,
And the balsam-groves and the poppy-fields
    That stretch on ever and ever so far.

The dream forests rustle their secrets out,
    The lights of the dream towns twinkle and shine,
And the white dream ships from the harbor sail
    Away to the dim horizon-line.

Ah! the sounds of the Valley are growing faint;
    Its sights are fading on either hand.
I cross the border still and dark,
    And enter the real Slumberland.

THE DREAMER.

When I am sleeping in my bed,
The little people in my head
All sport and frolic, dance and play,
As they never do by day.

They play at being king and queen,
Or catching fairy-folk unseen;
They act out giant, troll, or gnome,
Or in far Afric's forests roam.

They go with Sindbad on his trips,
Or take command of pirate ships,
And capture galleons of Spain,
Pearl-freighted, on the Spanish Main.

Yet each one still pretends he's me,
While I am sound asleep, you see;
They play I run and shout and leap—
And yet I'm lying fast asleep.

They have such jolly lots of fun,
And see such sights !   Yet never one
Will wake me up that I may go
To share the joys that please them so.

And if I wake and try to hear,
Or at their frolics try to peer,
Then all the sly things in a trice
Are quiet and demure as mice !

BEDTIME FANCIES.

Out from the corners and over the floor
   Come flocking and flocking the shadow band;
I will get in my little white coach and drive
   Through the Valley of Dreams into Slumberland.

I have four black horses that Night has lent;
   I call the name of my coachman Sleep;
And the little white coach is cozy and soft,
   As I nestle down in its cushions deep.

Heigh-ho! we are off.   The horses go slow
   At first, then fast and faster still,
With silent hoof-beats speeding on,
   Down to the foot of the Drowsy Hill.

This twilight place is the Valley of Dreams,
   Where all the wonderful dream things are,
And the balsam-groves and the poppy-fields
   That stretch on ever and ever so far.

The dream forests rustle their secrets out,
   The lights of the dream towns twinkle and shine,
And the white dream ships from the harbor sail
   Away to the dim horizon-line.

Ah! the sounds of the Valley are growing faint;
   Its sights are fading on either hand.
I cross the border still and dark,
   And enter the real Slumberland.

THE DREAMER.

When I am sleeping in my bed,
The little people in my head
All sport and frolic, dance and play,
As they never do by day.

They play at being king and queen,
Or catching fairy-folk unseen ;
They act out giant, troll, or gnome,
Or in far Afric's forests roam.

They go with Sindbad on his trips,
Or take command of pirate ships,
And capture galleons of Spain,
Pearl-freighted, on the Spanish Main.

Yet each one still pretends he's me,
While I am sound asleep, you see ;
They play I run and shout and leap—
And yet I'm lying fast asleep.

They have such jolly lots of fun,
And see such sights !   Yet never one
Will wake me up that I may go
To share the joys that please them so.

And if I wake and try to hear,
Or at their frolics try to peer,
Then all the sly things in a trice
Are quiet and demure as mice !

EPILOGUE.

The best of things, as well as the worst, must, like everything else, come to an end. We have had our say, and have done what we can to entertain you. If we have tried your patience it has been our misfortune, not our fault; and in the name of our little company I apologize for our shortcomings.

But, judging by the applause with which you have so generously rewarded some of us this evening, I think we have succeeded in amusing you; and your kind approval will encourage us to try to do still better next time.

As a parting word, we give you our hearty thanks for not only your presence here, but especially for your kind attention and encouragement. We say *au revoir*, but not good-by, with the hope to meet again some other time. Friends, one and all, good-night!

WHO BIDES HIS TIME.

Who bides his time, and day by day
   Faces defeat full patiently,
And lifts a mirthful roundelay
   However poor his fortunes be,
He will not fail in any qualm
   Of poverty; the paltry dime
It will grow golden in his palm—
   Who bides his time.

Who bides his time, he tastes the sweet
  Of honey in the saltest tear;
And though he fares with slowest feet,
  Joy runs to meet him, drawing near;
The birds are heralds of his cause,
  And, like a never-ending rhyme,
The roadsides bloom in his applause—
    Who bides his time.

Who bides his time, and fevers not
  In the hot race that none achieves,
Shall wear cool-wreathen laurel, wrought
  With crimson berries in the leaves;
And he shall reign a goodly king,
  And sway his hand o'er every clime,
With peace writ on his signet-ring—
    Who bides his time.

GRANDPA'S WAY.

My grandpa is the strangest man!
  Of course I love him dearly,
But really it does seem to me
  He looks at things so queerly.

He always thinks that every day
  Is right, no matter whether
It rains or snows, or shines or blows,
  Or what the kind of weather.

When outdoor fun is ruined by
  A heavy shower provoking,
He pats my head, and says, "You see,
  The dry earth needs a soaking."

And when I think the day too warm
  For any kind of pleasure,
He says, "The corn has grown an inch—
  I see without a measure."

And when I fret because the wind
  Has set my things all whirring,
He looks at me, and says, "Tut! tut!
  This close air needs a stirring!"

He says, when drifts are piling high,
  And fence-posts scarcely peeping,
"How warm beneath their blanket white
  The little flowers are keeping!"

Sometimes I think, when on his face
  His sweet smile shines so clearly,
It would be nice if every one
  Could see things just so queerly!

ESCAPING A SHOWER.

Two crabs who were out on the beach to walk
Shook claws when they met, and stopped to talk.

"We're going to have a storm," one said;
"Just look at those big clouds overhead!"

"Then if we stay," said the other, "it's plain
That both of us will be caught in the rain."

So, ere the threatened shower began,
Back in the water they quickly ran.

SUMMER SONG.

Hear the quail in yonder glen;
  He is calling to his mate;
You can hear him in the morning—
  Hear him early, hear him late.
    "Whistle! whistle!"
That is what the quail is saying
  As he whistles to his mate.

Hear the owl in yonder tree,
  Among the leaves so green;
Can you tell me what he's saying
  In his leafy house unseen?
    "Whoo! whoo!"
This is what the owl is saying
  In his leafy house unseen.

Seeking for his morning food
  See the crow in yonder field;

He must feed his little nestlings,
In the nest so well concealed.
" Caw ! caw ! "
This is what the crow is saying,
Seeking for his nestlings' food.

When the evening comes again,
And the earth in night is hid,
All along the woods and meadows
You can hear the katydid.
"Katydid ! katydid !"
All along the woods and meadows
You can hear the katydid.

WHEN I'M A MAN.

Oh, when I'm a man
Just as big as papa,
I'll have a mustache,
And I'll smoke a cigar.

I'll wear a tail-coat—
Oh, won't I be grand,
With a glass in my eye,
And a cane in my hand !

I'll buy all the papers,
And read all the news—
The *Times* and the *Standard*,
And weekly reviews.

And I'll have a birthday—
　　Just listen and hear—
About every week,
　　And not once a year.

And it would be better
　　If Christmas day came
A little bit oftener,
　　And New Year the same.

I'll be *very* rich;
　　For you'll certainly find
I'll run to the toy-shop
　　Whenever inclined.

I won't have a nurse-maid
　　To bother me so,
Nor teacher for lessons—
　　Oh dear, no, no, no !

Nor will I to bed,
　　Like a baby so small,
At seven o'clock—
　　No, I won't go at all !

Nasty rice-pudding,
　　Potatoes and meat,
Thick bread and butter,
　　I never will eat;

But dine on sweet candies
  Wherever I be,
With sponge-cakes for breakfast
And toffee for tea.

THE LAND OF MAKE-BELIEVE.

Have you ever heard of the wonderful land,
  The dear land of Make-believe,
Where the rivers have beds of golden sand,
And the clouds all day are rainbow-spanned;
Where every good girl at a word's command
May summon a beautiful fairy band
  And bid them new wonders weave ?
Oh, nowhere has earth, with all her noise,
Such a glorious spot for the little boys,
  Where never they fret or grieve,
As the kingdom known since the world was planned
  As the land of Make-believe.

Have you heard who own all the houses and things
  In the land of Make-believe ?
Why, sweet little fairies with silver wings,
Wearing satin slippers and diamond rings.
And they say, every time the south wind brings
Good boys and girls, the fairy queen sings,
And takes them all down to the honey springs
  If they never, never deceive ;

But then, if the children grow very bad,
The fairy queen becomes silent and sad,
 And folds her feathers to leave,
After tying the boys in her apron-strings,
 In the land of Make-believe.

In this wonderful land far over the seas,
 In the land of Make-believe,
They have candy horses and candy trees;
And the candy cows are taking their ease,
Lashing their tails in the peppermint breeze,
Or standing around right up to their knees
 Where the taffy billows heave.
There the kittens all fly—they never climb;
Everything has a magnificent time,
 As happy as Adam and Eve,
And every story comes out as you please,
 In the land of Make-believe.

BEES.

Folkses, do you think I look very green?
I'll tell you what—I've seen a queen!
Not the kind that wears long satin trails,
But that goes buzzing and buzzing around rails
And other things, for nice, fresh honey!

I've seen a king too—a real bee king!
Tell you what, folks, he's a queer thing!

When his subjects are indoors he proudly sits on the
    throne;
But when on a journey the queen leads off alone,
And they all follow to a tree that's hollow.

But the strangest thing—and it's true too;
My father told me so three days ago—
Is that bees can make honey; 'spect that's the why
I don't want any of 'em buzzing around me—do
    you?
Now my story 'bout bees is through.

WASHINGTON'S BIRTHDAY.

The bells of Mount Vernon are ringing to-day,
    And what say their melodious numbers
To the flag-blooming air? List! what do they say?—
    "The fame of the hero ne'er slumbers!"

The world's monument stands the Potomac beside,
    And what says the shaft to the river?—
"When the hero has lived for his country, and died,
    Death crowns him a hero forever."

The bards crown the heroes, and children rehearse
    The songs that give heroes to story;
And what say the bards to the children?—"No
    verse
    Can yet measure Washington's glory.

" For Freedom outlives the old crowns of the earth,
  And Freedom shall triumph forever,
And time must long wait the true song of his birth,
  Who sleeps by the beautiful river."

WHICH IS BEST?

A DIALOGUE FOR NINE BOYS.

Characters.

Boy,	Tinker,	Doctor,
Soldier,	Tailor,	Gentleman,
Sailor,	Plowboy,	Thief.

BOY (*dressed in coat with eight buttons*).

I wonder, when I'm bigger,
  What I would like to be—
A soldier with a helmet,
  Or a sailor on the sea ?
I think a soldier's nicest—
  Then you can have a gun,
And sometimes they let soldiers
  Play on a great big drum !

(*Enter boy dressed as* SOLDIER, *with drum.*)

SOLDIER.

You ought to be a soldier,
  And get a drum, you see (*shows drum*)
Just listen to my rub-dub (*beats drum*),
  And come and fight with me (*marches about*).

(*Enter* SAILOR, *dressed in uniform, small boat in hand.*)

SAILOR.

No, no; you be a sailor,
    And visit far-off lands,
And come back to your mother
    With strange things in your hands (*shows*
                    shells, coral, etc.).

(*Enter* TINKER, *with mended kettle in hand.*)

TINKER.

The best of all's a tinker,
    Who mends old pots and pans;
And since "ifs" aren't "kettles,"
    There's need for tinkers' cans.

(*Enter* TAILOR, *with large needle, who sits down cross-legged and begins to sew.*)

TAILOR.

You come and be a tailor—
    That's useful work, you know;
Who'd make and mend your jackets
    If tailors couldn't sew (*points to jacket*)?

(*Enter* PLOWBOY, *cracking long whip.*)

PLOWBOY.

Crack, crack! just hear my good whip!
    And I have horses too;
And plowing is so easy,
    It would just do for you.

(*Enter* DOCTOR, *with medicine bottle.*)

DOCTOR.

My work's to give folks physic (*uncorks bottle*),
    For which they dearly pay;
But I've to work at night-time,
    As well as through the day.

(*Enter* GENTLEMAN, *with hands in pockets.*)

GENTLEMAN.

I don't have to work any,
    Either by night or day;
For I have plenty money (*takes money from
                     pockets*)
    For everything to pay.

(*Enter, while* GENTLEMAN *is speaking,* THIEF, *in
ragged clothing.   Steals* GENTLEMAN'S *handker-
chief from pocket.*)

THIEF.

Ha, ha ! my fine young boaster !
    See what I got from you (*waves handker-
                    chief*) !
Although I don't work, either,
    I've plenty money too (*shows small coins*).

BOY (*considering*).

I'd like to be a soldier (*turns to* SOLDIER),
    But then I'd go with joy

To learn to be a sailor (*turns to* SAILOR),
　Or even a plowboy (*points to* PLOWBOY).
I'll have to count my buttons,
　And see what they've to say;
For if I have to choose here,
　I'll not be done to-day.
(*Counts buttons, repeating " Soldier, sailor," etc.*)
I've counted all my buttons,
　And have to say, with grief,
If I'm to do their bidding
　I've got to be a thief.

PROLOGUE.

FOR A BOY.

Did you ever, any of you, see the sun rise ? Have
you seen its first morning rays illumine and bring out
bright and clear everything that was dark and gloomy
in the shades of night, and make you feel glad that
you are alive ?

How funny it would seem for the sun to rise late
in the evening—about this time, for instance ! But
it does to-night, and I'll tell you how and why. It
is just this way: the manager of these solemnities,
naturally selecting the smartest of the young martyrs
under his control, said to me, " Son, you must rise to-
night—rise to the occasion—and make the opening
speech." You see what a mess of it I am making;

but I *have* risen, as you perceive, and I wish you all
heartily welcome. Having thus tried to brighten you
with my presence, and dispel your gloom of expecta-
tion and suspense, this son will now set—setting a
good example for those who are to follow by doing
my best to worry you as little as possible, and to try
to make you glad you came.

MAKING B'LIEVE.

I've maked b'lieve I was mama,
   And been to the bargain store;
But the bargain (the baby) wiggled so
   That I couldn't play that any more.
I've maked b'lieve I was C'lumbus,
   And discovered the world all over;
The rug was the 'Lantic Ocean,
   And I sailed on the nursery sofa.

I've maked b'lieve I was an Indian,
   And scalped Polyphemia twice;
And I played be a big polar bear,
   With the looking-glass for ice.
I've maked b'lieve I was the doctor,
   With pearl tapioca pills;
But I was 'bliged to give up practice,
   'Cause I couldn't c'lect my bills.

Two times I've b'lieved to be a circus,
    And two times the coal-man too;
And once I was Robinson Crusoe,
    And once I was little Boy Blue.
Oh, I've maked b'lieve and I've maked b'lieve,
    Till there's nothing else to be !
And now—I'm so hungry, mama—
    Let's make b'lieve I was me.

VALEDICTORY.

FOR A SMALL BOY.

Our exercises for the day
Will close without much more delay.
We thank you for the interest
Your kind attention has expressed.
We know we are but young and weak
To stand before a crowd to speak;
But mighty *oaks* from *acorns* grow,
And some of us, for aught you know,
May climb the noble hill of Fame,
And make a great and lasting name;
While none of us, we hope, may live
To loving hearts one pain to give.
Again we tender thanks to you;
Till next we meet, kind friends, adieu !

LITTLE MIDGET.

FOR A VERY LITTLE GIRL.

My papa sometimes scolds and says
    I'm always in a fidget !
But mama says I keep quite still
    For such a little midget ;

And teacher said to-day she thought
    That it was very smart
For such a little thing as I
    To learn a speech by heart.

THE MESSAGE OF THE SEASONS.

A RECITATION FOR FOUR GIRLS.

FIRST GIRL.

Behold the bright and smiling Spring !
    I set the brooklets free ;
The snowdrop-bells I gaily ring
    Across the sunny lea ;
I chase the dreary clouds of gloom
    That wrapped the earth so long,
I bid the flow'rets rise and bloom,
    I tune the skylark's song.

I hang the boughs with blossoms fair
   That promise fruit at last;
And in the gardens everywhere
   The seeds of hope are cast.
O boys and girls ! in goodness grow,
   For habits closely cling;
Take care, take care what seeds you sow
   Now in life's golden Spring !

SECOND GIRL.

See Summer like a fairy queen
   Awaken roses round !
Red, white, and pink, they wreathe the scene,
   And pansies gem the ground;
The royal lily, clad in white,
   Lifts up her stately head,
And dancing beams of golden light
   O'er grassy hills are shed.

The wavelets of the summer sea
   Sing out a glad refrain,
The bees go humming drowsily
   Across the heather plain.
O friends, in Summer's welcome glow
   We'll seek the fountain's brink;
We'll quench our thirst where waters flow,
   And not in fiery drink !

THIRD GIRL.

Now Autumn comes with ripe, ripe wheat,
   And bearded barley too;
And grapes are bending, dark and sweet,
   The smiling vineyards through;
The oats are waving in the breeze,
   But soon they'll be low laid;
The apples burn upon the trees,
   The nuts hang in the glade.

Oh, never crush the barley fair,
   That bloweth brown and free,
Into the ale-cup's hidden snare,
   That drags to misery;
Change not the oats that brightly shine
   To whisky's fatal blight,
Nor press the grapes to mocking wine,
   But use God's gifts *aright.*

FOURTH GIRL.

Now Winter ends the seasons' train,
   And shivers in the cold !
There's frost upon the window-pane,
   There's snow on hill and wold;
The hungry robin hops anear
   With timid, fluttering wing—
But Christmas comes, and glad New Year,
   And joy doth Winter bring.

Now friend meets friend,[1] and hearts are warm,
    And smiling looks abound;
You're sheltered safe from chilling storm,
    Where laugh and song go round.
And some will urge, "A glass you'll take,
    To keep you from the cold!"
Oh, for your feebler brethren's sake,
    Your pledge of temperance hold!

ALL.

Whate'er the season chance to be—
    In Spring or Summer glow,
When Autumn plenty crowns the lea,
    Or winds of Winter blow—
Stand free, stand free, while life shall last,
    From chains of sin and fear;
Oh, hold your pledge of temperance fast
    Through all the changing year!

THE BOY'S SERMON.

I came to-night to try to preach
    A sermon, if I can;
For little boys can preach to boys
    As well as men to men.

---

[1] No. 1 here shakes hands with No. 2, and No. 3 with No. 4.

I never thought of such a thing
   Until the other day;
I found a text so short and good,
   So hear to what I say.

"Mind" is my text; 'tis for you, boys,
   And something that you need.
The girls may listen to it all,
   And, what they ought to, heed !

First: *mind your tongue !* Don't let it speak
   An angry, an unkind,
A cruel, or a wicked word;
   Don't let it, boys; now mind !

Mind eyes and ears ! Don't even look
   At wicked books or boys;
From wicked pictures turn away—
   All sinful acts despise.

And *mind your lips !* Tobacco stains !
   Strong drink, too, keep away;
And let no bad words pass your lips—
   Mind everything you say.

Mind hands and feet ! Don't let them do
   A single wicked thing;
Don't steal or strike, don't kick or fight,
   Don't walk in paths of sin.

But more than all, oh, *mind your heart!*
From Satan turn aside;
Ask Jesus *there* to make His throne,
And ever there abide.

A BABY'S SOLILOQUY.

I am here. And if this is what they call the *world*, I don't think much of it. It's a very flannelly world, and smells of paregoric awfully. It's a dreadful light world, too, and makes me blink, I tell you. And I don't know what to do with my hands; I think I'll dig my fists in my eyes. No, I won't. I'll scratch at the corner of my blanket and chew it up, and then I'll holler; whatever happens, I'll holler. And the more paregoric they give me, the louder I'll yell. That old nurse puts the spoon in the corner of my mouth, sidewise like, and keeps tasting my milk herself all the while. She spilled snuff in it last night, and when I hollered she trotted me. That comes of being a two-days-old baby. Never mind; when I'm a man I'll pay her back good. There's a pin sticking in me now, and if I say a word about it, I'll be trotted or fed; and I would rather have catnip-tea. I'll tell you who I am—I found out to-day; I heard folks say, " Hush! don't wake up Emeline's baby;" and I suppose that pretty, white-faced woman over on the pillow is Emeline.

No, I was mistaken; for a chap was in here just now and wanted to see Bob's baby; and looked at me and said I was a funny little toad, and looked just like Bob. He smelled of cigars. I wonder who else I belong to! Yes, there's another one—that's "gamma." "It was gamma's baby, so it was." I declare, I do not know who I belong to; but I'll holler, and maybe I'll find out. There comes snuffy with catnip-tea. I'm going to sleep. I wonder why my hands won't go where I want them to!

MY SHADOW.

I have a little shadow
    That goes in and out with me;
And what can be the use of him
    Is more than I can see.

He is very, very like me,
    From the heels up to the head;
And I see him jump before me
    When I jump into my bed.

The funniest thing about him
    Is the way he likes to grow—
Not at all like proper children,
    Which is always very slow;

For he sometimes shoots up taller,
   Like an india-rubber ball;
And he sometimes gets so little
   That there's none of him at all!

He hasn't got a notion
   Of how children ought to play,
And can only make a fool of me
   In every sort of way.

He stays so close beside me,
   He's a coward you can see;
I'd think shame to stick to nursie
   As that shadow sticks to me

One morning, very early,
   Before the sun was up,
I rose, and found the shining dew
   On every buttercup;

But my lazy little shadow,
   Like an arrant sleepyhead,
Had stayed at home behind me
   And was fast asleep in bed.

GOOD-MORNING, MERRY SUNSHINE.

" Good-morning, merry sunshine!
   How did you wake so soon?

You've scared the little stars away,
   And shined away the moon.
I saw you go to sleep last night
   Before I ceased my playing;
How did you get 'way over there,
   And where have you been staying ? "

" I never go to sleep, dear child;
   I just go round to see
My little children of the East,
   Who rise and watch for me.
I waken all the birds and bees
   And flowers on my way;
And last of all, the little child
   Who stayed out late to play."

WHAT TO DRINK.

I think that every mother's son,
   And every father's daughter,
Should drink, at least till twenty-one,
   Just nothing but cold water;
And after that they might drink tea,
   But nothing any stronger.
If all folks would agree with me,
   They'd live a great deal longer.

OCTOBER'S PARTY.

October gave a party;
  The leaves by hundreds came—
The Chestnuts, Oaks, and Maples,
  And leaves of every name.
The sunshine spread a carpet,
  And everything was grand;
Miss Weather led the dancing,
  Professor Wind the band.

The Chestnuts came in yellow,
  The Oaks in crimson drest;
The lovely Misses Maple,
  In scarlet, looked their best.
All balanced to their partners,
  And gaily fluttered by;
The sight was like a rainbow
  New-fallen from the sky.

Then in the rusty hollows
  At hide-and-seek they played;
The party closed at sundown,
  And everybody stayed.
Professor Wind played louder;
  They flew along the ground;
And there the party ended
  In "hands across, all round."

RING HAPPY BELLS.

Ring, happy bells of Eastertime !
The world is glad to hear your chime;
  Across wide fields of melting snow
  The winds of summer softly blow,
And birds and streams repeat the chime
    Of Eastertime.

Ring, happy bells of Eastertime !
The world takes up your chant sublime:
  "The Lord is risen !" The night of fear
  Has passed away, and heaven draws near;
We breathe the air of that blest clime
    At Eastertime.

Ring, happy bells of Eastertime !
Our happy hearts give back your chime.
  The Lord is risen ! We die no more !
  He opens wide the heavenly door;
He meets us while to Him we climb
    At Eastertime.

AN APRIL FOOL.

"Welcome, pretty sunshine !"
  The dainty violet said,
As from beneath her leaflets green
  She lifts her little head.

"All my friends are fast asleep;
　　Please let them slumber yet,
For though you shine so bright and warm,
　　The ground is cold and wet."

The buttercup, soft slumbering still,
　　Now dreams that summer's here,
And, wakened by the April sun,
　　Believes no frost is near.

And heedless of the violet's voice—
　　Whose warning words foretell
Of April's frowns as well as smiles:
　　"For flowers 'tis not well"—

And thinking oft, as children do,
　　When they their ways will rule,
The flower peeped, and finding frost,
　　Sighed, "I'm an April fool!"

THE CHURCH SPIDER.

Two spiders—so the story goes—
　　Upon a living bent,
Entered the meeting-house one day,
And hopefully were heard to say,
"Here we shall have at least fair play,
　　With nothing to prevent."

Each chose his place and went to work;
    The light webs grew apace.
One on the sofa spun his thread,
But shortly came the sexton dread
And swept him off; and so, half dead,
    He sought another place.

" I'll try the pulpit next," said he—
    " There surely is a prize;
The desk appears so neat and clean,
I'm sure no spider there has been;
Besides, how often have I seen
    The pastor brushing flies ! "

He tried the pulpit, but, alas !
    His hopes proved visionary ;
With dusting-brush the sexton came,
And spoilt his geometric game,
Nor gave him time nor space to claim
    The right of sanctuary.

At length, half starved and weak and lean,
    He sought his former neighbor,
Who now had grown so sleek and round
He weighed the fraction of a pound,
And looked as if the art he'd found
    Of living without labor.

" How is it, friend," he asked, " that I
    Endured such thumps and knocks,

While you have grown so very gross ? "
" 'Tis plain," he answered ; " not a loss
I've met since first I spun across
　　The *contribution box*."

SEPTEMBER.

The goldenrod is yellow,
　　The corn is turning brown,
The trees in apple-orchards
　　With fruit are bending down ;

The gentian's bluest fringes
　　Are curling in the sun ;
In dusky pods the milkweed
　　Its hidden silk has spun ;

The sedges flaunt their harvest
　　In every meadow nook,
And asters by the brook-side
　　Make asters in the brook.

By all these lovely tokens
　　September days are here,
With summer's best of weather
　　And autumn's best of cheer.

THE MICE.

The merry mice stay in their holes
    And hide themselves by day;
But when the house is still at night,
    The rogues come out and play.

Now here, now there, they trot about;
    In every hole they peep,
To see what they can find to eat
    While we are fast asleep.

They taste of milk we set for cream,
    And nibble bread and cheese;
They climb upon the pantry shelf,
    And taste of all they please.

But if they chance to hear the cat,
    Their feast will soon be done;
Off, off they go to hide themselves,
    As fast as they can run.

THE COW.

The friendly cow, all red and white,
    I love with all my heart;
She gives me milk with all her might,
    To eat with apple-tart.

She wanders lowing here and there—
  And yet she cannot stray—
All in the pleasant open air,
  The pleasant light of day.

And blown by all the winds that pass,
  And wet with all the showers,
She walks among the meadow-grass,
  And eats the meadow-flowers.

THE FOUR SEASONS.

A RECITATION FOR FOUR CHILDREN.

(*If desired, the children may be dressed in character.*)

FIRST CHILD.

My name is Spring; I bring warm showers,
  And many a gentle breeze,
And crocuses and daffodils,
  And buds on all the trees.

SECOND CHILD.

My name is Summer; in my hands
  I bring the sweetest flowers,
And leafy trees, and long, warm days,
  And sunny, golden hours.

THIRD CHILD.

My name is Autumn; in my time
  I bring the ripened corn,
And gayest flowers and richest fruit,
  And frosty eve and morn.

FOURTH CHILD.

My name is Winter; when I come
  I lay the plants to sleep,
And cover them from wind and frost,
  With snowy mantle deep.

FIRST CHILD.

When I draw near, the little lambs
  Begin to bleat and play;
And birds begin to sing and build,
  And longer grows the day.

SECOND CHILD.

When I draw near, the farmer sends
  His men to cut the grass;
O'er all the land the scent of hay
  Blows sweetly as I pass.

THIRD CHILD.

When I draw near, to reap the corn
  The merry reapers go;
The farmer stores his roots and grain
  Before the winter's snow.

FOURTH CHILD.

When I draw near, the fields are bare,
   But fires more brightly burn;
And gentle hearts with kindly help
   To poor and needy turn.
I bring the joyful Christmas-tide,
   The happiest in the year;
So, spite of all my gloom and cold,
   The children hold me dear.

ALL.

We come with ever-varying gifts
   And ever-changing faces;
But One who never changes sets
   Our duties and our places.
Not one alone, but all alike,
   We do His blessed will;
By heat and cold, by sun and shower,
   We seasons serve Him still.

LITTLE HELPERS.

RECITATION FOR A LITTLE GIRL.

Washing and wiping the dishes,
   Bringing in wood from the shed,
Ironing, sweeping, and dusting,
   Trying to make well our bed,

Taking good care of the baby,
   Watching her lest she might fall—
We little children are busy,
   For there is work for us all.

Reading the paper for grandma,
   Who sits by the stove busy knitting,
Setting the table for supper,
   Or on errands fast we're flitting;
Driving the cows to the pasture,
   Feeding the horse in the stall,
We little children are busy—
   Yes, there is work for us all.

A SERMON IN RHYME.

If you have a friend worth loving,
   Love him. Yes, and let him know
That you love him, ere life's evening
   Tinge his brow with sunset glow.
Why should good words ne'er be said
Of a friend—till he is dead ?

If you hear a song that thrills you,
   Sung by any child of song,
Praise it. Do not let the singer
   Wait deservèd praises long.
Why should one who thrills your heart
Lack the joy you may impart ?

If you hear a prayer that moves you
   By its humble, pleading tone,
Join it.   Do not let the seeker
   Bow before his God alone.
Why should not your brother share
The strength of " two or three " in prayer ?

Scatter ever seeds of kindness,
   All enriching as you go ;
Leave them.   Trust the Harvest-giver—
   He will make each seed to grow ;
And until its happy end
Your life shall never lack a friend.

Dick & Fitzgerald

PUBLISHERS,

18 ANN STREET,

Post Office Box 2975.   NEW YORK.

Upon receipt of the price, any books advertised in the following pages will be sent by mail, postage paid, to any Post Office in the United States, Canada, and the Universal Postal Union.

No Books Exchanged.   **No Books sent C. O. D.**

Not Responsible for Money or Books sent by Mail, unless Registered.

Parcels will be registered on receipt of Ten Cents in addition to the amount of the order.

Under no Circumstances will Books be sent Subject to Approval.

No Orders whatever will be Filled unless sufficient money accompanies them.

Write your name plainly.

Give full Address, with Post Office, County and State.

A complete descriptive Catalogue will be mailed free on application.

HOW TO SEND MONEY.

In remitting by mail the safest means are a Post-office or Express Money Order, or a Draft on a New York Bank, payable to Dick & Fitzgerald. When these are not procurable, Cash (or a Postal Note) should be sent in a Registered Letter. Unused United States Postage Stamps, of the denomination of Ten Cents or under, will be taken as cash in amounts less than One Dollar. Soiled Stamps, Postage Stamps other than those of the United States, and personal checks or drafts on local banks cannot be accepted

FOR VERY LITTLE CHILDREN.

Little Lines for Little Speakers. Containing short and easy Pieces for Children, entirely new and original, suitable for Juvenile Exhibitions and Entertainments. By Clara J. Denton. For convenience in making selections, the First Part contains short and easy pieces for boys and girls of seven to ten years of age ; in the Second Part are shorter and easier pieces for little children ranging from four to seven years ; the Third Part consists of pieces for Special Occasions, such as First and Last day of School, Thanksgiving, Christmas, Easter, Washington's Birthday, Fourth of July, Weddings, Salutatory and Valedictory Speeches, etc. The Pieces are prominently notable for their originality, simplicity, and effective humor. Paper covers...15 cts.

Dick's Little Speeches for Little Speakers. Containing original and Selected Recitations, bright, easy, and effective, well adapted for Young Children and little Tots, and suitable for Children's Entertainments of every description. This little book offers a variety of over one hundred patriotic, serious, instructive and humorous pieces for boys and girls, very carefully selected and exceedingly effective, ranging from pieces of one or two simple couplets for the four-year-old pets, to the more pretentious Recitations for children of ten years of age, easily memorized, and suitable for general and special occasions. Paper covers......15 cts.

Dick's Little Dialogues for Little People. Consisting of Original and Selected Dialogues specially adapted for performance by Young and quite young children in Sunday School and other Juvenile Entertainments. The Dialogues range from the very easiest and simplest for very small children to those suitable for girls and boys of nine or ten years of age, in which some dramatic scope is introduced, but entirely within their capabilities ; including also Dialogues for Patriotic occasions, for opening and closing Anniversary Exhibitions, and others requiring a number of speakers for their performance. Some of the Dialogues are on serious and instructive subjects, but the majority are full of sparkling wit and effective humor. Paper covers............................15 cts.

Dick's Choice Pieces for Little Children. A Collection of real nice little Speeches, original and selected, and just the thing for Young Children in School Exhibitions and other Juvenile Entertainments. The pieces are mainly short and easily memorized, suitable for boys and girls from four to ten years of age ; including selections appropriate for Arbor Day, Christmas and other special occasions; also a short Christmas Pantomime for quite little children, and Prologues and Epilogues specially adapted for young people. Some of the pieces are original, and all are bright and entertaining. Paper covers............................15 cts.

Holmes' Very Little Dialogues for Very Little Folks. Containing forty-seven new and original Dialogues, with short and easy parts, mainly in words of one syllable and entirely suited to the capacity and comprehension of very young children. By Alice Holmes. The short conversations combine good moral tone with a great deal of humor, and are suitable for any entertainment in which very small children take part. It contains a very amusing piece for Santa Claus and a large number of little tots. Paper covers.................................30 cts.

Kavanaugh's Comic Dialogues and Pieces for Little Children. Comprising short and easy original pieces for Sunday School and other exhibitions. By Mrs. Russell Kavanaugh. This book includes several amusing Christmas Pieces, introducing a novel Christmas Tree in which twenty-one little girls take part; a complete set of speeches for representing the different festivals during the year; a Floral Festival for twelve performers ; and a great number of Dialogues and Recitations entirely suitable for young and very small boys and girls. Every thing is written in the simplest style, easily learned and comprehended by young children. Paper covers.................................30 cts.

MODEL SPEECHES AND SKELETON ESSAYS.

Ogden's Model Speeches for all School Occasions.

Containing Original Addresses and Orations on everything appertaining to School Life; comprising Set Speeches on all occasions connected with Schools, Academies and Colleges, for School Officers, as well as for Teachers and Students of both sexes, with appropriate replies. By Christol Ogden.

This original work contains over one-hundred telling speeches and replies in well-chosen words, and every variety of style, for

All Kinds of School Ceremonials.	*Burlesque Speeches.*
Speeches on Opening and Dedicating New Schools and Academies.	*Addresses to Teachers.*
Salutatory and Valedictory Addresses.	*Prologues and Epilogues for School Exhibitions.*
Presentations and Conferring Honors.	*Anniversary Congratulations.*

Including practical hints on Extempore speaking with a dissertation on the selection of appropriate topics, suitable style, and effective delivery, and also valuable advice to those who lack confidence when addressing the Public. Paper..**50 cts.**

Bound in boards..**75 cts.**

Ogden's Skeleton Essays; or Authorship in Outline.

Consisting of Condensed Treatises on popular subjects, with references to sources of information, and directions how to enlarge them into Essays, or expand them into Lectures. Fully elucidated by example as well as precept. By Christol Ogden.

In this work is a thorough analysis of some SEVENTY prominent and popular subjects, with extended specimens of the method of enlarging them into Essays and Lectures.

The following interesting topics are separately and ably argued on both sides of the question, thus presenting also well digested matter for Debate, being on subjects of absorbing interest everywhere :—

Bi-Metalism.	*The Credit System.*
Civil Service Reform.	*Free Trade and Protection.*
Prohibition.	*Capital Punishment.*
Is Marriage a Failure?	*Shall More or Less be Taught in*
City and Country.	*Public Schools.*

All the remaining subjects are equally thoroughly discussed, and form a valuable aid to the student in preparing compositions, essays, etc.

Paper..**50 cts.**

Bound in boards..**75 cts.**

Dick's Book of Toasts, Speeches and Responses.

Containing Toasts and Sentiments for Public and Social Occasions, and specimen Speeches with appropriate replies suitable for the following occasions:

Public Dinners.	*Friendly Meetings.*
Social Dinners.	*Weddings and their Anniversaries.*
Convivial Gatherings.	*Army and Navy Banquets.*
Art and Professional Banquets.	*Patriotic and Political Occasions.*
Agricultural and Commercial Festivals.	*Trades' Unions and Dinners.*
Special Toasts for Ladies.	*Benedicts' and Bachelors' Banquets.*
Christmas, Thanksgiving and other Festivals.	*Masonic Celebrations.*
	All Kinds of Occasions.

This work includes an instructive dissertation on the Art of making amusing After-dinner Speeches, giving hints and directions by the aid of which persons with only ordinary intelligence can make an entertaining and telling speech. Also, Correct Rules and Advice for Presiding at Table.

The use of this work will render a poor and diffident speaker fluent and witty—and a good speaker better and wittier, besides affording an immense fund of anecdotes, wit and wisdom, and other serviceable matter to draw upon at will. Paper...**30 cts.**

Bound in boards...**50 cts.**

Frost's Dialogues for Young Folks.

A Collection of Origi. nal, Moral and Humorous Dialogues. Adapted to the use of School and Church Exhibitions, Family Gatherings and Juvenile Celebrations on all Occasions. By S. A. Frost.

CONTENTS.	Boys.	Girls.	CONTENTS.	Boys.	Girls.
Novel Reading	1	1	A Place for Everything	2	2
The Bound Girl		4	I Want to be a Soldier	2	
Writing a Letter		2	Self-Denial	2	3
The Wonderful Scholar	1	2	The Traveler	3	
Slang	4		Idleness the Mother of Evil		4
The Language of Flowers		4	The French Lesson	5	
The Morning Call		4	Civility Never Lost	3	2
The Spoiled Child		4	Who Works the Hardest?	1	1
The Little Travelers	2	2	The Everlasting Talker		5
Little Things	1	1	The Epicure	3	
Generosity		2	True Charity	1	7
Country Cousins		4	Starting in Life	1	1
Winning the Prize		2	I Didn't Mean Anything	4	
The Unfortunate Scholar		4	Ambition	5	
The Day of Misfortunes	3		Choosing a Trade	9	
Jealousy	1	3	The Schoolmaster Abroad	7	
The May Queen		5	White Lies	3	
Temptation Resisted	3		The Hoyden	1	3

16mo, Paper Covers. Price.................................30 cts.
Bound in Boards.................................50 cts.

Frost's New Book of Dialogues.

A series of entirely new and original humorous Dialogues, specially adapted for performance at School Anniversaries and Exhibitions, or other Festivals and Celebrations of the Young Folks.

CONTENTS.	Boys.	Girls.	CONTENTS.	Boys.	Girls.
Slang versus Dictionary	3		The Intelligence Office	4	3
Country or City		3	Cats	6	
Turning the Tables	3		Too Fine and Too Plain		3
The Force of Imagination		4	The Fourth of July Oration	5	
The Modern Robinson Crusoe	5		The Sewing Circle		7
The Threatened Visit		3	Fix	2	
The Dandy and the Boor	3		The Yankee Aunt	2	3
Nature versus Education		4	The Walking Encyclopedia	5	
The British Lion and Ameri-			The Novel Readers		3
can Hoosier	3		The Model Farmer	2	
Curing a Pedant		5	Buying a Sewing-Machine	4	2
Pursuit of Knowledge under			Sam Weller's Valentine	2	
Difficulties	2		The Hungry Traveler	2	
The Daily Governess		2	Deaf as a Post	1	2
The Army and Navy	2	2	The Rehearsal	6	
Economy is Wealth		3			

These Dialogues are admirably adapted for home performance, as they require no set scenery for their representation. By S. A. Frost. 180 pages, 16mo.

Paper covers. Price.................................30 cts.
Bound in boards, cloth back.................................50 cts.

McBride's New Dialogues.
Specially designed for School and Literary Entertainments. Entirely new and introducing eccentric and dialect characters. By H. Elliott McBride.

CONTENTS.	Boys.	Girls.	CONTENTS.	Boys.	Girls.
A Happy Woman	3	1	A Shoemaker's Troubles	4	1
The Somnambulist	5	1	The Opening Speech	6	
Those Thompsons	1	1	The Cucumber-Hill Debating		
Playing School	8		Club	6	
Tom and Sally	2	2	Married by the New Justice	3	1
Assisting Hezekiah	2	1	Bread on the Waters	1	1
A Visit to the Oil Regions	4	2	An Unsuccessful Advance	1	1
Breaking up the Exhibition	6		When Women Have Their		
Turning Around	4		Rights	2	1
A Little Boys' Debate	4		Only Another Footprint	5	1
The Silver Lining	1	2	Rosabella's Lover	4	1
Restraining Jotham	5	4	A Smart Boy	2	1
An Uncomfortable Predica-			A Heavy Shower	2	3
ment	2	3	Master of the Situation	2	1

Illuminated paper covers. Price......................30 cts.
Bound in boards...................................50 cts.

McBride's Temperance Dialogues.
Intended for the use of Schools, Temperance Societies and Home Performance, introducing various dialect characters. By H. Elliott McBride.

CONTENTS.	Boys.	Girls.	CONTENTS.	Boys	Girls.
Acting Drunk	4		Ralph Coleman's Reformation	4	3
Banishing the Bitters	8	1	Barney's Resolution	1	1
The Poisoned Darkies	3		Commencing to Work	3	
A Meeting of Liquor Dealers	5		A Temperance Meeting	7	
Out of the Depths	5	2	The Closing of "The Eagle"	4	2
The March of Intemperance	3	1	Don't Marry a Drunkard to Re-		
Maud's Command	2	3	form Him	8	3
A Beer-Drinker's Courtship	3	1	Obtaining a Promise	1	1

Illuminated paper covers. Price......................30 cts.
Bound in boards...................................50 cts

McBride's Humorous Dialogues.
Designed for School Exhibitions and Juvenile Entertainments. By H. Elliott McBride. Entirely original and full of humor and eccentricities.

CONTENTS.	Boys.	Girls.	CONTENTS.	Boys.	Girls.
Striking the Blow	1	4	A Boys' Meeting	5	
Curing the Borrowers	3	3	A Happy Family	3	2
Another Arrangement	2	2	A Farmers' Meeting	6	
Scene in the Bobtown School	9		Uncle Sam's Wars	7	1
Mrs. Bolivar's Quilting		6	Riches Have Wings	3	3
A Rumpus		4	The Reclaimed Father	5	1
Scene in a Railway Station	4	2	Leaving Jonah	3	1
A Pantaloon Fight	1	2			

Illuminated paper covers. Price......................30 cts.
Bound in Boards...................................50 cts.

Kavanaugh's Juvenile Speaker. For very little boys and girls. Containing short and easily-learned Speeches and Dialogues, expressly adapted for School Celebrations, May-Day Festivals and other Children's Entertainments. By Mrs. Russell Kavanaugh. This book is just the thing for Teachers, as it gives a great number of short pieces for children from five to ten years of age, with directions for appropriate dresses.

It contains nearly fifty Speeches and Recitations ; besides the following attractive Dialogues :

	Boys.	Girls.		Boys.	Girls.
Opening Song................		13	The Love-Scrape..............	2	1
Opening Recitation..	1	12	An Old Ballad.............	1	1
An Interrupted Recitation.....	1	1	The Milkmaid.	1	1
A Joyful Surprise.............	3	2	Billy Grimes, the Drover... ..		2
How He Had Him......	2	1	Honesty the Best Policy.....	4	
Poetry, Prose, and Fact.	1	2	Baby Bye................		4
Small Pitchers have Large Ears		2	Helping Papa and Mamma....	2	2
The Young Critic.............	2		The Little Mushrooms........		3

It includes a complete May-Day Festival, with opening chorus and appropriate speeches for nineteen boys and girls.

It introduces the May-Pole Dance, plainly described, and forming a very attractive and pleasing exhibition.

16mo, Illuminated Paper Cover. Price.............**30 cts.**
16mo, Boards.......................................**50 cts.**

Kavanaugh's Exhibition Reciter, for Very Little Children. A collection of entirely Original Recitations, Dialogues, and Short Speeches, adapted for very little boys and girls ; including also a variety of pieces, Humorous, Serious, and Dramatic, suitable for children from three to ten years old, for Public and Private School Exhibitions and other Juvenile Entertainments. It contains over fifty Speeches and Recitations for single performers, and in concert ; and the following Dialogues :

	Boys.	Girls.		Boys.	Girls.
The Gipsy's Warning.	1	2	The Fairy's Revenge	3	15
The Power of Justice..........	1	9	An Old-Time Breakdown......	5	5
The Months...........	3	9			
The Four Queens..............	2	4	—		
Repartee	1	1	MUSIC.		
The Midgets' Greeting.	1	1	The Gipsy's Warning.........		
The Five Wishes........		6	Jewels Bright................		
Poor Old Maids....		6	Baby Fair...		
The Old Year Out and the New			Gentle Zitella................		
Year In....................	6	6	Tell Me, Where do Fairies		
Scene from "Robin Hood."...	6		Dwell ?		

It also includes a May-Day Festival for very little children, and a number of beautiful Speaking Tableaux. By the author of "Kavanaugh's Juvenile Speaker."

Bound in Illuminated Paper Covers...................**30 cts.**
Bound in Illuminated Board Covers..................**50 cts.**

Dick's Dutch, French and Yankee Dialect Recitations.

An unsurpassed Collection of Droll Dutch Blunders, Frenchmen's Funny Mistakes, and Ludicrous and Extravagant Yankee Yarns, each Recitation being in its own dialect.

DUTCH DIALECT.

Der Mule Shtood on der Steambond Deck.
Go Vay, Becky Miller.
Der Drummer.
Mygel Snyder's Barty.
Snyder's Nose.
Dyin' Vords of Isaac.
Fritz und I.
Betsey und I Hafe Bust Ub.
Schneider sees Leah.
Dot Funny Leetle Baby.
Schnitzerl's Philosopede.
Der Dog und der Lobster.
Schlosser's Ride.
Mine Katrine.
Maud Muller.
Ein Deutsches Lied.
Hans and Fritz.
Schneider's Tomatoes.
Deitsche Advertisement.
Vas Bender Henshpecked.
Life, Liberty and Lager.
Der Goot Lookin' Shnow.
Mr. Schmidt's Mistake.
Home Again.
Dot Surprise Party.
Der Wreck of der Hezberns.
Isaac Rosenthal on the Chinese Question.
Hans Breltmann's Party.
Shoo Flies.
A Dutchman's Answer.
How Jake Schneider Went Blind.
I Vash so Glad I Vash Here.
The Dutchman and the Yankee.
How the Dutchman Killed the Woodchuck.
Der Nighd Pehind Grisdmas.
The Dutchman's Snake.
Yoppy's Varder und Hees Drubbles.
Dhree Shkaders.
Katrina Likes Me Poody Vell.
Hans in a Fix.
Leedle Yawcob Strauss.
How a Dutchman was Done.
Dot Lambs vot Mary Haf Got.
The Yankee and the Dutchman's Dog.
Zwei Lager.
Schneider's Ride.
The Dutchman and the Small-pox.
Tiamondts on der Prain.
A Dutchman's Testimony in a Steamboat Case.
Hans Breitmann and the Turners.

FRENCH DIALECT.

The Frenchman's Dilemma; or, Number Five Collect Street.
The Frenchman's Revenge.
Noozell and the Organ Grinder.
How a Frenchman Entertained John Bull.
Mr. Rogers and Monsieur Denise.
The Frenchman and the Landlord.
The Frenchman and the Sheep's Trotters.
A Frenchman's Account of the Fall.
I Vant to Fly.
The Generous Frenchman.
The Frenchman and the Flea Powder.
The Frenchman and the Rats.
Monsieur Tonson.
Vat You Please.
The Frenchman and the Mosquitoes.
The Frenchman's Patent Screw.
The Frenchman's Mistake.
Monsieur Mocquard Between Two Fires.

YANKEE DIALECT.

Mrs. Bean's Courtship.
Hez and the Landlord.
Squire Billings' Pickerel.
Deacon Thrush in Meeting.
The Yankee Fireside.
Peter Sorgbum in Love.
Mrs. Smart Learns how to Skate.
Capt. Hurricane Jones on the Miracles.
The Dutchman and the Yankee.
The Yankee Landlord.
The Bewitched Clock.
The Yankee and the Dutchman's Dog.
Aunt Hetty on Matrimony.
The Courtin'.
Ebenezer on a Bust.
Sut Lovingood's Shirt.

This Collection contains all the best dialect pieces that are incidentally scattered through a large number of volumes of "Recitations and Readings," besides new and excellent sketches never before published. 170 pages, paper cover...............30 cts.
Bound in boards, cloth back...50 cts.

Dick's Irish Dialect Recitations. A carefully compiled Collection of Rare Irish Stories, Comic, Poetical and Prose Recitations, Humorous Letters and Funny Recitals, all told with the irresistible Humor of the Irish dialect. Containing

Biddy's Troubles.
Birth of St. Patrick, The.
Bridget O'Hoolegoin's Letter.
Connor.
Dermot O'Dowd.
Dick Macnamara's Matrimonial Adventures.
Dying Confession of Paddy M'Cabe.
Father Molloy.
Father Phil Blake's Collection.
Father Roach.
Fight of Hell-Kettle, The.
Handy Andy's Little Mistakes.
How Dennis Took the Pledge.
How Pat Saved his Bacon.
Irish Astronomy.
Irish Coquetry.
Irish Drummer, The.
Irish Letter, An.
Irish Philosopher, The.
Irish Traveler, The.
Irishman's Panorama, The.
Jimmy McBride's Letter.
Jimmy Butler and the Owl
King O'Toole and St. Kevin.
Kitty Malone.
Love in the Kitchen.
Micky Free and the Priest.
Miss Malony on the Chinese Question.
Mr. O'Hoolahan's Mistake.
Paddy Blake's Echo.
Paddy Fagan's Pedigree.
Paddy McGrath and the Bear.
Paddy O'Rafther.
Paddy the Piper.
Paddy's Dream.
Pat and the Fox.
Pat and the Gridiron.
Pat and his Musket.
Pat and the Oysters.
Pat's Criticism.
Pat's Letter.
Pat O'Flanigan's Colt.
Patrick O'Rouke and the Frogs.
Paudeen O'Rafferty's Say Voyage.
Peter Mulrooney and the Black Filly.
Phaidrig Crohoore.
Rory O'More's Present to the Priest.
St. Kevin.
Teddy O'Toole's Six Bulls.
Wake of Tim O'Hara, The.
Widow Cummiskey, The.

This Collection contains, in addition to new and original pieces, all the very best Recitations in the Irish dialect that can be gathered from a whole library of "Recitation" books. It is full of sparkling witticisms and it furnishes also a fund of entertaining matter for perusal in leisure moments. 170 pages, paper cover...............30 cts.
Bound in boards, cloth back...50 cts.

Tambo's End-Men's Minstrel Gags. Containing some of the

best Jokes and Repartees of the most celebrated "burnt cork" performers of our day. Tambo and Bones in all sorts and manner of scrapes. This Book is full of Burnt-Cork Drolleries, Funny Stories, Colored Conundrums, Gags and Witty Repartee, all the newest side-splitting conversations between Tambo, Bones, and the Interlocutor, and will be found useful alike to the professional and amateur performer. Contents:

A Bird that can't be Plucked
Annihilating Time
At Last
Bashful
Bet, The
Big Fortune, A
Blackberrying
Black Swan, The
Bones and his little Game
Bones and the Monkey Tricks
Bones as a Fortune Teller
Bones as a Legitimate Actor
Bones as a Pilot
Bones as a Prize Fighter
Bones as a "Stugent"
Bones as a Traveler
Bones as a Victim to the Pen
Bones as a Walkist
Bones assists at the Performance of a New Piece
Bones attends a Seance
Bones finds Himself Famous
Bones gets Dunned
Bones gets Stuck
Bones has a Small Game with the Parson
Bones' Horse Race
Bones in an Affair of Honor
Bones in Love
Bones keeps a Boarding House
Bones on the War Path
Bones on George Washington
Bones on the Light Fantastic

Bones Opens a Spout Shop
Bones Plays O'Fella
Bones sees a Ghost
Bones Slopes with Sukey Sly
Bones tells a "Fly" Story
Brother will come home to-night
Bones as a Carpet Bagger
Bones as an Inkslinger
Bones in a New Character
Bones in Clover
Bones' Love Scrape
"Cullud" Ball, The
Conundrums
Curious Boy
Dancing Mad
Dat's What I'd Like to Know
Definitions
De Mudder of Inwention
Difference, The
Don't Kiss every Puppy
"Far Away in Alabam'"
First White Man, The
Fishy Argument
Four-Eleven-Forty-Four
Four Meetings, The
From the Polks
Girl at the Sewing Machine
Hard Times
Hard to take a Hint
Heavy Spell, A
Highfalutin'
Horrible!
How Bones became a Minstrel
How Tambo took his Bitters
How to do it

Impulsive Oration
Inquisitive
Jealousest of her Sect
Legal Problem, A
Liberal Discount for Cash
Manager in a Fix, The
Mathematics
Merry Life, A
Momentous Question
Mosquitoes
Music
Notes
Ob Course
Our Shop Girls
Pomp and Ephy Green
Presidency on de Brain
Proposed Increase of Taxes
Railroad Catastrophe
Reality versus Romance
Rough on Tambo
Sassy Sam and Susie Long
School's In
Shakespeare with a Vengeance
Simple Sum in Arithmetic
Sleighing in the Park
Sliding Down the Hill
Style
Sublime
Swearing by Proxy
Tambo's Traveling Agent
That Dear Old Home
"The Pervisions, Josiar"
Thieves
Tonsorial
Toast, A
Uncle Eph's Lament
Waiting to See Him Off
You Bet
And 40 popular songs and dances.

Everything new and rich. Paper covers • • • • • • • • • • 30cts.
Bound in boards, with cloth back • • • • • • • • • • • 50cts.

McBride's Comic Speeches and Recitations. Designed for

Schools, Literary and Social Circles. By H. Elliott McBride, Author of "McBride's Humorous Dialogues," etc., etc. This is one of the very best series of original speeches, in Yankee, Darkey, Spread-Eagle and village styles, with a number of diverting addresses and recitations, and funny stories, forming an excellent volume of selections for supplying the humorous element of an exhibition. Contents:

A Burst of Indignation
Disco'se by a Colored Man
A Trumpet Sarmon
Sarmon on Skilletvillers
Nancy Matilda Jones
Hezekiah's Proposal
About the Billikinses
Betsy and I are Out Once More
A Stump Speech
About Katharine
Deborah Doolittle's Speech on Women's Rights
A Salutatory
A Mournful Story

An Address to Schoolboys
Zachariah Popp's Courtship and Marriage
A Sad Story
How to Make Hasty Pudding
My Matilda Jane
Courtship, Marriage, Separation and Reunion
Lecture by a Yankee
A Colored Man's Disco'se on Different Subjects
A Girl's Address to Boys
McSwinger's Fate

Peter Peabody's Stump Speech
Mr. Styx Rejoices on Account of a New Well Spring
Victuals and Drink
Speech by Billy Higgins on the Destruction of His Rambo Apple Tree
A Boy's Address to Young Ladies
An Old Man's Address to Young Wives
Salu-ta-tat-u-a-ry Valedictory.

Paper covers, illuminated • • • • • • • • • • • 30cts.
Board covers illuminated • • • • • • • • • • • 50cts.

Beecher's Recitations and Readings. Humorous, Serious,

Dramatic. Designed for Public and Private Exhibitions. Contents:

Miss Maloney at the Dentist's	The Cry of the Children	Signor Billsmethi's Dancing Academy
Lost and Found	The Dutchman and the Small-pox	Der Goot Lookin Shnow
Mygel Snyder's Barty	Sculpin	The Jumping Frog
Magdalena	Rats—Descriptive Recitation	The Lost Chord
Jim Wolfe and the Cats		The Tale of a Leg
The Woolen Doll	A Reader Introduces Himself to an Audience	That West-side Dog
The Charity Dinner		How Dennis Took the Pledge
Go-Morrow; or, Lots Wife	A Dutchman's Dolly Varden	
The Wind and the Moon		The Fisherman's Summons
Dyin' Words of Isaac	"Rock of Ages"	Badger's Debut as Hamlet
Maude Muller in Dutch	Feeding the Black Fillies	Hezekiah Stole the Spoons
Moses the Sassy	The Hornet	Paddy's Dream
Yarn of the "Nancy Bell"	The Glove and the Lions	Victuals and Drink
Paddy the Piper	I Vant to Fly	How Jake Schneider Went Blind
Schneider sees "Leah"	That Dog of Jim Smiley's	
Caldwell of Springfield	The Faithful Soul	Aurelia's Young Man
Artemus Ward's Panorama	"My New Pittayatees"	Mrs. Brown on Modern Houses
Tale of a Servant Girl	Mary Ann's Wedding	
How a Frenchman Entertained John Bull	An Inquiring Yankee	Farm Yard Song
	The Three Bells	Murphy's Pork Barrel
Tiamondts on der Prain	Love in a Balloon	The Prayer Seeker
King Robert of Sicily	Mrs. Brown on the Streets	An Extraordinary Phenomenon
Gloverson the Mormon	Shoo Flies	
Do Pint wid Ole Pete	Discourse by the Rev. Mr. Bosan	The Case of Young Bangs
Pat and the Pig		A Mule Ride in Florida
The Widow Bedott's Letter	Without the Children	Dhree Shkaders

Paper covers. Price - - - - - - - - - - - 30cts.
Bound in boards, cloth back - - - - - - - - - - 50cts.

Dick's Ethiopian Scenes, Variety Sketches and Stump

Speeches. Containing the following Rich Collection of Negro Dialogues, Scenes, Farces, End-Men's Jokes, Gags, Rollicking Stories, Excruciating Conundrums, Questions and Answers for Bones, Tambo and Interlocutor, etc. Contents:

I's Gwine to Jine de Masons	Speech on Boils	Brudder Bones in Clover
Jes' Nail dat Mink to de Stable Do'—Oration	How Bones Cured a Smoky Chimney	Artemus Ward's Advice to Husbands
But the Villain still Pursued Her—A Thrilling Tale	Sermon on Keards, Hosses, Fiddlers, etc.	Where the Lion Roareth, and the Wang-Doodle Mourneth
	Huggin' Lamp-Posts	
	Not Opposed to Matrimony	Romeo and Juliet in 1880
Bones at a Free-and-Easy	How Pat Sold a Dutchman	Artemus Ward's Panorama
Buncombe Speech	The Coopers—one Act Farce	Brudder Bones as a Carpet-Bagger—Interlocutor and Bones
Shakespeare Improved	Questions Easily Answered—Bones and Tambo	
End Gag—Bones and Tambo		
A Man of Nerve—Comic Sketch	Examination in Natural History—Minstrel Dialogue	Major Jones' Fourth of July Oration
End Gag—Bones and Tambo	O'Quirk's Sinecure	Curiosities for a Museum—Minstrel Dialogue
Uncle Pete—Darkey Sketch	The Widower's Speech	Burlesque Oration on Matrimony
The Rival Darkeys	Bones at a Raffle	
The Stage-Struck Darkey	Uncle Pete's Sermon	Brudder Bones on the Raging Canawl
Add Ryman's Fourth of July Oration	Bones at a Soiree—Interlocutor and Bones	The Snackin'-Turtle Man—Ethiopian Sketch
Absent-Mindedness—Bones and Tambo	Speech on Woman's Rights	
	Bones' Discovery	Bones' Dream—Ethiopian Sketch
Don't Call a Man a Liar	Mark Twain Introduces Himself — Characteristic Speech	Come and Hug Me
The Mysterious Darkey		Widow O'Brien's Toast
Rev. Uncle Jim's Sermon	Speech on Happiness	Scenes at the Police Court—Musical Minstrel Dialogue
The 'Possum-Run Debating Society	Burnt Corkers—Minstrel Dialogue	
Tim Murphy's Irish Stew	Tue Nervous Woman	Brudder Bones as a Log-Roller
Brudder Bones in Love—Interlocutor and Bones	The Five Senses—Minstrel Dialogue	De Pint Wid Old Pete—Negro Dialect Recitation
'Lixey; or, The Old Gum Game—Negro Scene	The Dutchman's Experience	A Touching Appeal—Dutch Dialect Recitation
Brudder Bones' Duel	Essay on the Wheelbarrow	Wounded in the Corners Darkey Dialogue
Brudder Bones' Sweetheart	Bones at a Pic-Nic	
Brudder Bones in Hard Luck	The Virginia Mummy—Negro Farce	End Gag—Interlocutor and Bones
Two Left-Bones and Tambo		

178 pages, paper covers - - - - - - - - - - - - 30cts.
Bound in board, cloth back - - - - - - - - - - - 50cts.

Kavanaugh's New Speeches and Dialogues for Young Children.

Containing easy pieces in plain language, readily understood by little children, and expressly adapted for School Exhibitions and Christmas and other juvenile celebrations. By Mrs. Russell Kavanaugh. This is an entirely new series of Recitations and Dialogues by this author, and full of pieces, in her well-known style of familiar simplicity, admirably calculated to give the little ones additional opportunities to distinguish themselves before an audience. It contains the following:

Title	Girls	Boys
Introduction		
Opening Speech		1
Speech for a School Exhibition		1
The Parcæ (The Fates)	3	
Which Would You Rather Be?	6	
Speech for a Tiny Girl	1	
An Old Story, for a Child		
Speech for a Boy		1
A Sudden Revulsion		
Mr. and Mrs. Santa Claus. A Novel Christmas Festival		2
May Celebration	8	3
Speech of Crowner	1	
Speech of Sceptre-Bearer	1	
Speech of Fun	1	
Speech of Frolic	1	
Speech of Vanity	1	
Speech of Modesty	1	
Speech of Beauty	1	
Speech of Jollity		1
Speech of Boot-Black		1
Speech of News-Boy		1
Speech of May-Queen	1	
The Tables Turned, for a Child		
Speech for a Boy		1
Speech for a Small Boy		1
Speech for a Very Little Boy		1
The Farmer Boy and the City Dude		2
The Small boy	1	
Transposed	1	
The Sun and His Satellites	7	
Speech of the Sun	1	
Speech of the Moon	1	
Speech of Mercury	1	
Speech of Mars	1	
Speech of Jupiter	1	
Speech of Saturn	1	
Speech of Venus	1	
True Happiness		1
Genius and Application	2	
Five Versus Twenty-five		1
Saved from Suicide		1
Speech for a Very Small Child		
Three Enigmas	3	
Tickle his Hand with a Ten Dollar Bill		1
Speech for a Small Boy		1
Beautiful Belles, for several Girls		
Beautiful Dudes, for several Boys		
Four Little Rose-Buds	4	
A Bouquet	12	
Ta! Ta!		1
Speech for a Very Little Girl	1	
Speech for a Very Little Boy		1
Blood Will Tell		1
A Warning		1
A Race for Life		1
"He is a Brick"		1
Speech for a Small Boy		1
Watching	1	
Gold		1
A Touching Incident		1
Buy a Broom, for several Girls		
Confusion Worse Confounded		1
A Relentless Tyrant, for a Child		
My Brother Jean	1	
The Gratitude of the World		
At the Skating Rink		1
Dimes! Oh, Dimes!		1
A Fatal Bait, for a Child		
The Decorated Donkey, for a Child		
Tight Times		1
The Reason Why		
A Modern Flirtation		
Country Meeting Talk		2
Speech		1
Deeds of Kindness		
The Boy's Complaint		1
What Not to Do		
Temperance Address		1
The Quarrelsome Boy		1
An Awful Fly, for a Little One		
Content	1	
The Winds of the Prairie		
Santa Claus' Christmas Tree Speech		1
The Creator		
Where Did They Go	1	
The Parting Lovers	1	1
Do Your Best		1
Cherish Kindly Feelings		
Advice to Boys	1	
I Wish I Was a Grown-up		1
No Time Like the Present		
The Boys We Need		1
Summer Vacation	1	
MUSIC.		
Three Bright Stars		
Beautiful Belles		
Buy a Broom		

16mo. Illuminated Paper Cover.....30 cts. Boards.............50 cts.

Howard's Recitations. Comic, Serious and Pathetic.

Collection of fresh Recitations in Prose and Poetry, suitable for Anniversaries, Exhibitions, Social Gatherings, and Evening Parties. Contents:

Miss Malony on the Chinese Question
Kit Carson's Ride
Buck Fanshaw's Funeral
Knocked About
Puzzled Dutchman
Shamus O'Brien
Naughty Little Girl
Bells of Shandon
No Sect in Heaven
Rory O'Moore's Present
"Mother's Fool"
Queen Elizabeth—a Comic Oration
The Starling
Lord Dundreary's Riddle
The Stuttering Lass
The Irish Traveler
The Remedy as Bad as the Disease
A Subject for Dissection
The Heathen Chinee
Mona's Waters
A Showman on the Woodchuck
How Happy I'll Be
A Frenchman's Account of the Fall
Isabel's Grave
Parson and the Spaniel

An Irishman's Letter
Irish Letter
The Halibut in Love
The Merry Soap-Boiler
The Unbeliever
The Voices at the Throne
Dundreary Proposing
The Fireman
Paul Revere's Ride
Annie and Willie's Prayer
A Frenchman on Macbeth
The New Church Organ
Katrina Likes me Poudy Vell
How to Save a Thousand Pounds
How I Got Invited to Dinner
Patient Joe
Jimmy Butler and the Owl
The Menagerie
Old Quizzle
Infidel and Quaker
The Lawyer and the Chimney-Sweeper
Bill Mason's Bride
Judging by Appearances
The Death's Head
Betsey and I are Out
Betsey Destroys the Paper
Father Blake's Collection
Blank Verse in Rhyme

Roguery Taught
Banty Tim
Antony and Cleopatra
Deacon Hezekiah
The Frenchman and the Landlord
The Family Quarrel—A Dialogue on the Sixteenth Amendment
The Guess
Atheist and Acorn
Brother Watkins
Hans in a Fix
To-Morrow
The Highgate Butcher
The Lucky Call
Challenging the Foreman
Country Schoolmaster
The Matrimonial Bugs and the Travelers
Peter Sorghum in Love
Tim Tuff
Nick Van Stann
The Debating Society
Deacon Stokes
To Our Honored Dead
The Dying Soldier
The Yankee Fireside
The Suicidal Cat
The Son's Wish

16 mo. 180 pages. Paper covers. Price........................**30 cts.**
Bound in boards, cloth back........................**50 cts.**

Spencer's Book of Comic Speeches and Humorous Recitations

A collection of Comic Speeches and Dialogues, Dramatic Scenes and Characteristic Soliloquies and Stories Suitable for School Exhibitions. Contents:

Comic Prologue and Introduction
The Yankee Landlord
His Eye was Stern
The Goddess of Slang
Dick, the Apprentice
Courting in French Hollow
The Case Altered
Fox and the Ranger
The Declaration
The Warrantee Deed
A Night's Adventure
Julia—Comic Love Scene
Saying not Meaning
Negro Burlesque for 3 males
The Nimmers
Gucom and the Back-log
Widow Bedott's Mistake
How a Bashful Lover "Popped the Question"
Crossing Dixie
My Last Shirt
The Three Black Crows
The Barber's Shop
Paddy O'Raftfier
Decidedly Coo

Frenchman and the Rats
The Jester Condemned to Death
Kindred Quacks
Hans Breitmann's Party
The Generous Frenchman
Saint Jonathan
Stump Speech
The Rival Lodgers
The Frenchman and the Mosquitoes
The Maiden's Mishap
The Removal
Talking Latin
Praying for Rain
Darkey Photographor
Paddy and his Musket
Hezekiah Bedott
Uncle Reuben's Tale
Mr. Caudle has been to a Fair
Chemist and his Love
Disgusted Dutchman
The Frightened Traveler
Jewess and her Son
Clerical Wit—True Lies

The School House
Daniel versus Dishclout
Spectacles
The Pig
A Stray Parrot
Dame Fredegonde
Toby Tosspot
Courtship and Matrimony
Rings and Seals
The Biter Bit
Pat and the Gridiron
Barmecide's Feast
The Country Pedagogue
The Middle-aged Man and Two Widows
Saratoga Waiter—Negro Scene for 2 males
The Wrangling Pair—A Poetical Dialogue for Male and Female
A Connubial Eclogue
The Italian from Cork
Gasper Schnapps' Exploit
Epilogue—Suitable for Conclusion of an Entertainment

Paper covers. Price ....**30 cts.**
Bound in boards, cloth back........................**50 cts.**

Martine's Droll Dialogues and Laughable Recitations.

A collection of Humorous Dialogues, Comic Recitations and Spirited Stump Speeches and Farces, adapted for School and other Celebrations. Contents:

Hints to Amateur Actors.	The Darkey Debating Society. Dialogue for 2 males	The Poor Relation. Comic Drama for 7 males
Humorous Poetical Address	The Scandal Monger. Dialogue for 2 males and 2 females	Vat you Please
The Bell and the Gong		The Babes in the Wood. For 3 males and 4 females.
Mrs. Dove's Boarding House	Poor Richard's Sayings	My Aunt.
The Wilkins Family	Prologue to " The Apprentice "	Handy Andy's Mistakes.
The Lawyer's Stratagem	Address in the character of " Hope " A Prologue	The Cat Eater.
Eulogy on Laughing		A Shocking Mistake. Dialogue for 3 males and 2 females
Drawing a Long Bow. For 3 males and 1 female.	Parody on the Declaration of Independence	Wanted a Governess
The Origin of Woman's Ascendency over Man	Bombastes Furioso. A Burlesque for 7 males	Rival Broom Makers
Veny Raynor's Bear Story		Paudeen O'Rafferty's Say-Voyage
The Game of Life	Characteristic Address	Mr. Caudle's Wedding Dinner
The Fortune Hunter. For 2 males and 3 females	Examining de Bumps. Ethiopian Dialogue for 2 males	Our Cousins. Negro Dialogue for 2 male characters
The Parson and the Widow	Election Stump Speech	Mr. Caudle made a Mason
Hezekiah Stubbins' Fourth of July Oration	A Matrimonial Tiff. Dialogue for 1 male and 2 females	Address of Sergeant Buzfuz
Make your Wills Farce for 7 male characters	The Frenchman and the Sheep's Trotters	The Wonderful Whalers
Mr. Rogers and Monsieur Denise		Sam Weller's Valentine
Job Trotter's Secret		

188 pages. Paper Covers. Price......................................30 cts.
Bound in Boards, cloth back...................................50 cts.

Wilson's Book of Recitations and Dialogues. Containing

a choice selection of Poetical and Prose Recitations. Designed as an Assistant to Teachers and Students in preparing Exhibitions. By Floyd B. Wilson, Professor of Elocution. Contents:

Instruction in Elocution	The Picket Guard	Charge of a Dutch Magistrate
Dedication of Gettysburg Cemetery	The Poor Man and the Fiend	Stars in my Country's Sky
Sheridan's Ride	Our Country's Call	Bingen on the Rhine
There's but one Pair of Stockings	The Conquered Banner	Religious Character of President Lincoln
	The High Tide ; or, the Brides of Enderby	
Modulation	Death of Gaudentis	The Raven
Drummer Boy's Burial	Don Garzia	The Loyal Legion
John Maynard, the Pilot	Past Meridian	Agnes and the Years
The Boys	The Founding of Gettysburg Monument	Cataline's Defiance
The Duel		Our Folks
Lochiel's Warning	Spartacus to the Gladiators	The Beautiful Snow
Socrates Snooks	Soliloquy of the Dying Alchemist	The Ambitious Youth
Mosaic Poetry		The Flag of Washington
Burial of the Champion of his Class at Yale College	The Country Justice	The Abbot of Waltham
Scott and the Veteran	Unjust National Acquisition	Ode to an Infant Son
Barbara Frietchie	Dimes and Dollars	The Scholar's Mission
I Wouldn't—Would You ?	Dead Drummer Boy	Claude Melnotte's Apology
The Professor Puzzled	Home	Forging of the Anchor
Thanatopsis	Responsibility of American Citizens	Wreck of the Hesperus
The Two Roads		The Man of Ross
The Pawnbroker's Shop	The Jester's Sermon	No Work the Hardest Work
The Sophomore's Soliloquy	Left on the Battle Field	What is Time ?
The Nation's Hymn	The American Flag	Brutus's Oration over the Body of Lucretia
Address to a Skeleton	Oh ! Why should the Spirit of Mortal be Proud ?	What is That, Mother ?
A Glass of Cold Water	Parrhasius	A Colloquy with Myself
Little Gretchen ; or New Year's Eve	The Vagabonds	St. Philip Neri and the Youth
	A Bridal Wine Cup	
Good News from Ghent	Blanche of Devan's Last Words	The Chameleon
The Sea Captain's Story	Widow Bedott to Elder Sniffles	Henry the Fourth's Soliloquy on Sleep
Our Heroes		On Procrastination
The Closing Year	A Psalm of the Union	Appendix
Burial of Little Nell		

Paper Covers. Price......................................30 cts.
Bound in Board, cloth back.................................50 cts.

Brudder Bones' Book of Stump Speeches and Burlesque

ORATIONS. Also containing Humorous Lectures, Ethiopian Dialogues, Plantation Scenes, Negro Farces and Burlesques, Laughable Interludes and Comic Recitations. Contents:

If I may so Speak. Burlesque Oration
Dr. Pillsbury's Lecture on Politics
Vegetable Poetry. For 2 males
Teco Brag's Lecture on Astronomy
Wo saw Her but a Moment
Stocks Up, Stocks Down. For 2 males
Brudder Bones' Love Scrapes.
Stump Speech; or, "Any other Man."
War's your Hoss. Dialogue Recital
Geology. Dialogue for 2 males
Tin-pan-o-ni-on. For Leader and Orchestra
Dr. Puff Stuff's Lecture on Patent Medicines
Sailing. For 2 males
Challenge Dance. For 3 males
Lecture on Bad Boys
Tony Pastor's Great Union Speech
A Tough Boarding House
Sleeping Child. 2 males
Ain't I Right, Eh? Speech
Wonderful Egg. For 2 males
Bootblack's Soliloquy
Lecture to a Fire Company

Julius' Peaches. For 2 males
De Trouble Begins at Nine
The Arkansas Traveler. For 2 Violin players
Slap Jack. For 2 Darkeys
Turkey - town Celebration. An Oration
Uncle Steve's Stump Speech
A Midnight Murder
Dat's What's de Matter
The Freezing Bed Feller
Mr. and Mrs. Wilkins
Paddy Fagan's Pedigree
The Rival Darkeys. Act for 2 males
Hans Sourcrout on Signs and Omens
Hun-ki-do-ris Fourth of July Oration
Josh Billings on Mosquitoes
History of Cap John Smith
A Speech on Women
Impulsive Peroration
The Bet. For 2 Darkeys
Old Times gone By. Dialogue for 2 Darkeys
The Echo. Act for 2 Negroes
Sol Slocum's Bugle.
Western Stump Speech
In the Show Business. Dialogue for 2 males
"We are." Stump Oration
Original Burlesque Oration
Waiting to see Him off. For 2 males

Patriotic Stump Speech
De Railroad Accident. For 2 Darkeys
The Dutchman's Lecture
Prof. Unworth's Lecture
The Three old Ladies
Josh Billings' Lecture onto Musick
Brudder Bones' Lady-Love. Dialogue for 2 males
Deaf—In a Horn. Act for 2 males
Or any oder Man's Dog. A Speech
Happy Uncle Tom
Stick a Pin Dere, Brudder Horace
Lecture on Woman's Rights
Dat's wot de "Ledger" says. For 2 Darkeys
Goose Hollow Stump Speech
De Milk in de Cocoa Nut
A Dutchman's Answer
Lecture on Cats
The Patent Screw
The Auctioneer
Hints on Courtship
Dutch Recruiting Officer
Spirit Rappings. Dialogue for 2 males
Dar's de Money
Let Her Rip. Burlesque Lecture
The Stranger. Scene for 1 male and 1 female

16 mo.   188 pages.   Paper covers.   Price.....................................30 cts.
Bound in boards, illuminated...50 cts.

Dick's Diverting Dialogues.

A collection of effective Dramatic Dialogues, written expressly for this work by various authors, and adapted for Parlor Performances. They are short, full of telling "situations," introducing easy dialect characters, and present the least possible difficulties in scenery and costume to render them exceedingly attractive. Edited by Wm. B. Dick.

	Girls.	Boys.		Girls.	Boys.
Lost and Won	2	2	A Society for Doing Good	4	
Running for Office		3	The Reception. A Proverb	2	3
The Uncle. A Proverb	1	2	Caught in their Own Trap	2	3
Love's Labor Not Lost	1	2	Elwood's Decision		4
Wanted—A Nurse	3	2	The Report. A Proverb	2	1
Almost A Tragedy		2	Reformed Mormon Tippler	3	1
The Will. A Proverb	1	3	The Fortune Hunter. A Proverb	2	2
Who Wears the Breeches	1	1	Petticoat Government	1	2
A Cold in the Head	4	2	Now or Never. A Proverb	1	3
The Wedding Day. A Proverb	1	3	A Close Shave		2

Including a complete programme of effective Living Portraits and Tableaux, with full directions for exhibiting them successfully.
Paper covers. Price. ....30 cts.
Bound in boards, with cloth back.........................50 cts.

Dick's Comic and Dialect Recitations.

A capital collection of Comic Recitations, Ludicrous Dialogues, Funny Stories, and Inimitable Dialect Pieces, containing:

An Æsthetic Housekeeper
At the Rug Auction
Aunt Sophronia Tabor at the Opera—Yankee Dialect
Awfully Lovely Philosophy
Bad Boy and the Limburger Cheese, The
Barbara Frietchie—Dutch
Boy in the Dime Museum
Bric-a-Brac
Brudder Johnson on 'Lectri-city—Negro Dialect
Butterwick's Weakness
By Special Request
Can this be True?
Champion Liar, The
Conversion of Colonel Quagg
Out, Cut Behind—Dutch
Debit and Credit in the Next World
Der Oak und der Vine
Der 'Sperience of Reb'rend Quacko Strong—Negro
Der Vater Mill
Doctor's Story,
Dutch Advertisement,
Dutchman and the Raven
Dutch Security—Dutch
Early Bird, The
Gentle Mule, The
Granny Whar You Gwine?
Girl of Culture,
Goin' Somewhere—Yankee

Go-Morrow, or Lot's Wife
Hard Witness, A
Horse that Wins the Race
How a Woman Does It
How Buck was Brought to Time—Yankee Dialect
How Uncle Fin had the Laugh on the Boys
Humming Top, The
In der Shweed Long Ago
Inquisitive Boy, The
Irishman's Perplexity, An
Jim Onderdonk's Sunday-School Oration
John Chinaman's Protest
Juvenile Inquisitor, A
Malony's Will—Irish Dialect
Mark Twain on the 19th Century
Mickey Feeny and the Priest
Mine Moder-in-Law
Mother's Doughnuts
Mr. and Mrs. Potterman
Mr. Schmidt's Mistake
Mr. Spoopendyke Hears Burglars
O'Branigan's Drill
Old Bill Stevens
Old Erasmus' Temperance Pledge—Negro Dialect
Ole Settlers' Meetun
Original Love Story, An
Our Debating Club

Parson Jinglejaw's Surprise
Pat's Correspondence
Pleasures of the Telephone
Positively the Last Perfor-mance—Cockney Dialect
Raven, The—Dutch Dialect
Sad Fate of a Policeman
Scripture Questions
Sermon for the Sisters, A
Solemn Book-Agent, The
That Fire at Nolan's
That Freckle-Faced Girl
The Latest Barbara Friet-chie—Dutch Dialect
The Paper Don't Say
Thikhead's New Year's Call
Tickled all On for
'Twas at Manhattan Beach
Uncle Billy's Disaster
Uncle Mellick Dines with his Master—Negro Dialect
Uncle Remus' Tar Baby
Uncle Reuben's Baptism
United Order of Half-Shells
Walter's Trials, A
Warning to Woman, A
Ways of Girls at the Play
Western Artist's Accom-plishments, A
Wily Bee, The
Woman's Description of a Play, A
Yaller Dog, The

Bound in Boards...30 cts.
Paper Covers..50 cts.

Barton's Comic Recitations and Humorous Dialogues.

Containing a variety of Comic Recitations in Prose and Poetry, Amusing Dialogues, Burlesque Scenes, Eccentric Orations, Humorous Interludes and Laughable Farces.

A Prologue to Open an En-tertainment
The Stage-Struck Hero
Here She Goes—and There She Goes
Pastor M'Knock's Address
Old Sugar's Courtship
The Bachelor's Reasons for Taking a Wife
The Spanish Valet and the Maid—Dialogue for 1 male and 1 Female.
The Jackdaw of Rheims
Jonathan and the English-man
Artemus Ward's Trip
Auctioneer and the Lawyer
Mr and Mrs. Skinner
The Bachelor and the Bride
Drunkard and his Wife
A Western Lawyer's Plea against the Fact
Reading a Tragedy
Cast-off Garments
How to Cure a Cough
The Soldier's Return
Countrymen and the Ass
Come and Go

How they Pop the Question
The Clever Idiot
The Knights
How the Lawyer got a Patron Saint
Josh Billings on Laughing
Night after Christmas
A Change of System—for 2 males and 1 female
Citizen and the Thieves
Bogg's Dogs
The Smack in School
The Tinker and the Miller's Daughter
An Original Parody
The Parsons and the Cork-screw
The Old Gentleman who Married a Young Wife—Stage-Struck Darkey—Inter-ludo for males
Goody Grim versus Lapstone—Dialogue for 4 males
The Woman of Mind
Wanted, a Confederate—Farce for 4 males
Lodgings for Single Gentle-men

Nursery Reminiscences
The Farmer and the Coun cellor
The Pugilists
How Pat Saved his Bacon
The Irish Drummer
Mike Hooter's Bear Story
The Critic
Mr. Caudle Wants a Latch Key
Humbugging a Tourist
The Widow's Victim—for 2 males and 1 female
Josh Billings on the Mule
Tinker and the Glazier
Wonderful Dream—Negro Dialogue for 2 males
An Occasional Address—For a Lady's First Appearance
An Occasional Prologue—For Opening a Perfor-mance
Address on Closing a Per-formance
A Prologue for a Perfor-mance by Boys
An Epilogue for a School Performance

Paper Covers. Price..30 cts.
Bound in Boards, cloth back...................................50 cts.

COMPLETE DESCRIPTIVE CATALOGUE MAILED FREE.

DICK & FITZGERALD, Publishers,

P. O. Box 2975,   New York.